CAPTURED

INNOCENCE

Cynthia Hickey

D1738219

Arise, O Lord, Deliver me, O my God!
strike all my enemies on the jaw;
break the teeth of the wicked

- Psalm 3:7..

ACKNOWLEDGMENTS

This story was one of my first, pulled back out of the drawer and updated. Thank you to all who remembered me writing it and asked that it be finished..

1

The night breeze carried whispers of her name.

Footsteps sounded behind her.

A chill coursed down her spine, prickling her skin with goose bumps.

Jocelyn Nielson pulled her ratty brown sweater tighter across her chest and risked another peek over her shoulder. She paused, and the echoing footfalls stopped. Maybe she'd imagined the sound in the first place. She didn't see anyone out of the ordinary. No one paid her undue attention. She raised a hand to her throat and took a deep breath. Her gaze swept the sidewalk.

A few older women window shopped, pointing, and gasping at prices. A young man stood on the corner to hail a taxi. His shrill whistle pierced Jo's ears. A group of teenage girls giggled as they ambled along the sidewalk and stopped under a streetlamp. They looked in compact mirrors or punched numbers into their brightly colored cell phones.

Jo examined their low rise jeans and designer tops. She smoothed the skirt of the full dress she wore and plucked at the sleeve of her button up sweater. Twenty-five, and she dressed like an old maid. She sighed. Someday—when she felt safe. Safe enough to believe her ex-husband wouldn't find her, then, she'd go on with her life. She'd wear pretty clothes again.

Quickening her pace, she stopped beneath the street lamp and checked her watch. Eight o'clock! She was late picking up Alex from the babysitter. Again. Why had she covered the other waitress's shift? She pressed her hand against her forehead. *Because I need the money, that's why*.

She darted to merge with the group of teenagers who assessed her with scornful looks and turned their attention back to each other. She walked with them for two blocks, marveling at their ability to chatter so animatedly and ignore her presence. When had she ever been so carefree?

A few minutes later, she left them and stopped in front of a dark alley. A short cut, it would shave fifteen minutes off her walk. She took another glance at her watch then scanned the sidewalk behind her. Her ears strained to hear sounds of pursuit. Nothing.

Taking a shaky breath, she stepped into the dimness of the alley. Every horror movie of stupid heroines ran through her mind. She shrugged. Making up the time she'd lost was more important. She couldn't afford to find another baby-sitter, and she'd been warned many times about being late.

The night wind tore down the alley. Jo's long hair whipped from her pony tail and around her face, obscuring her vision.

An aluminum can rattled.

Her heart leapt into her throat.

She froze, then spun and shoved her hair from her face. Her eyes scanned the darkness behind her.

The streetlight cast a yellow glow over the entrance to the alley. The figure of a man stood in silhouette, legs parted, hands held loosely at his sides. A trench coat flapped around his knees.

She gasped and ran--away from the light. Away from the stranger. Her breath rasped, and her heart pounded against her ribcage. The sound of her own frantic footsteps masked those of any would-be assailant.

A brick wall loomed.

Panic rioted through her as she whirled, searching for a place to hide. She ducked behind a dumpster and risked another glance down the alley. Her blood pounded in her ears.

There was no one to be seen. No sound of stalking feet. No cans rattled. Only the wind blew and whistled across several open lids of other dumpsters lining the alley.

Jo turned toward a scurrying sound. Red beady eyes stared at her from under a cardboard box. She screamed. A rat darted from its hiding place.

She rose, poised for flight like a wild animal who'd caught an unfamiliar scent. Her gaze darted from one corner of the alley to another, anxiously trying to find a way around the brick obstacle.

"Jocelyn." A soft, sinister voice sliced through her quickly unraveling nerves. It couldn't be him, could it? There could be no way he knew where she'd run to.

A cat leapt from the dumpster, and the lid rattled like distant thunder. Jo collapsed back onto a pile of garbage bags someone had neglected to dispose of.

"Jocelyn." The voice came again. Clearer. Louder.

She scrambled to her feet. Her shoes slipped on the rotten vegetable matter that oozed from the ripped bags.

A rancid smell assaulted her. Her hand plunged into a gooey substance. She shook it clean. A sob caught in her throat.

"What do you want with me?" Her voice came out as a hoarse whisper. "Please leave me alone."

The rising wind tangled her skirt around her legs. With one hand on her sweater, she tried holding down her skirt with the other.

The man seemed to have disappeared. He no longer called her name in that eerie sing-song way. His shadow no longer stretched down the alley.

She spotted a small gate to the right of the brick wall. She eased toward it, straining to listen for footsteps in pursuit. She glanced over her shoulder every few feet.

A bang, a crash, and a thud somewhere in the dark spurred her faster. She ran and resisted the urge to look back. Reaching the end of the alley, she turned right. The two blocks to her apartment building seemed like two miles.

Her shoes tapped out a beat as she half-ran, half-walked. Several people glanced her way, and she ducked her head to avoid their faces. Tears poured down her cheeks, and she swiped them away.

One man reached out to stop her. "Are you all right?" Jo halted and glanced up. Blue eyes locked with hers. The man stepped toward her. She squeaked in alarm and darted away from him.

"Wait," he called after her. "Let me help you?"

Jo glanced back. Her eyes were drawn to the tall man, lean, with massive shoulders. A scream bottled in her throat. She sprinted around the corner and burst through the gate to the fence circling her apartment building.

She put a hand to her chest. She wheezed like a squeaky screen door. Jo patted her pockets for her inhaler. Stupid! She'd left it upstairs in her apartment.

Risking one more look down the street, she rammed her key into the lock of the security door. Slipping inside, she closed the door and leaned against it, concentrating on regulating her breathing. Precious seconds ticked by before her breathing slowed. "I'm a fool," she whispered to herself. *Taking the alley as a shortcut.*

Taking the stairs two at a time, she used the railing to pull herself along, and came to a noisy stop outside her babysitter's apartment door. She took a deep breath. She still wheezed, but with less pain, and rang the bell.

"You're late." Mrs. Leonard frowned at her, her severe face drawn into disapproving wrinkles.

"I'm so sorry. I was held up at work." Jo transferred her attention to her five-year-old son who stood next to the babysitter. "Hey, baby. Sorry I'm late."

Alex gazed up at her with dark brown eyes, so like her own. They never failed to brighten Jo's day, no matter how hectic it had been. "That's okay, Mommy. You're here now."

Jo bent and kissed her son's cheek. "You're so sweet. I don't deserve you."

"You're squeaking," Alex said.

"I ran. Didn't want to be too late picking up my little man, did I? I'm okay."

Mrs. Leonard continued to stare down her nose at them, as if in silent agreement about Jo's statement of her unworthiness. Jo took a deep breath and straightened to meet the older woman's eyes.

"I told you what I would have to do if you were late again."

"I understand Mrs. Leonard, but..."

"You are not setting a good example for your son, Ms. Kingsley." Mrs. Leonard folded her thin arms across her flat chest. "Punctuality is a worthy trait."

"Please." Jo hated the pleading tone that crept

into her voice. "Alex is such a good boy. You've said he doesn't cause you a bit of trouble."

"That's beside the point. This happens too often. My time is valuable. I have a life besides caring for your son."

Jo's heart skipped a beat. "I'll pay you extra. I can't afford to lose you or my job. You have to realize I would never abandon my son." She squared her shoulders. "I'll pay you an extra ten dollars a week to cover any evenings I run late." *How will I ever afford it*?

Mrs. Leonard sniffed. "I don't like it. Being consistently late isn't good parenting."

Alex grasped the older woman's hand. "Please." He raised his eyes to hers and smiled.

A smile twitched at the corner of the other woman's mouth. "All right, Alex."

Jo relaxed her shoulders and took her son's hand. At least the woman had a soft spot for her son. "Let's get you to bed, sir."

Her son chattered non-stop as they climbed the two flights of stairs to their small one bedroom apartment. He regaled Jo with tales of what he'd learned in Kindergarten before the bus dropped him into Mrs. Leonard's care.

"What did you do with Mrs. Leonard today?"

Alex frowned. "She makes me do my homework first thing. Then I can watch cartoons. Sometimes I help her fold laundry."

"Laundry? Really?" Jo chuckled and unlocked the door to their apartment. She pulled the chain on the overhead light and grimaced as cockroaches scurried for cover. The landlord had promised her he would spray.

She spotted her inhaler on the kitchen table and grabbed it to take two puffs of the medication. She felt her bronchial tubes relax. "Come on, Alex. We have to see Mr. Every."

"I don't like him," Alex said. "He's mean. Like a stranger."

She looked at her son. "I agree, but we've got to be polite. Okay?"

"Okay." The little boy slid his hand into hers.

With a firm grasp on Alex's hand, Jo led the way down the three flights of steps to the first floor. She rapped on the door labeled 'Manager', then buttoned her sweater to the top button, covering the thin white blouse beneath.

"Jo." The man stunk of body sweat and beer. He wore faded black slacks and a stained, sleeveless tee shirt that strained to cover a large paunch, a ludicrous addition to his gaunt frame.

Jo wrinkled her nose and stepped back. "Mr. Every, there are still cockroaches in my apartment. You promised you would take care of them." She averted her eyes from the way he'd combed thinning hair slicked over to one side of his head in a vain attempt not to appear bald.

"Now, Jo." He stepped aside and flung an arm wide, inviting her inside. "Let's talk about this inside."

"There's nothing to talk about. You promised. A man's word should be concrete."

His eyes narrowed, and his gaze to ran slowly over her body. Jo clenched her fists at her side and struggled to remain where she stood and not shrink back. Her flesh crawled, and she mentally counted her loose change, estimating whether she had enough for a bath. The apartments shared several bathrooms, charging a dollar for each short shower.

"Jo, things could be so much easier for you if you'd only let me..."

"Besides the bugs, things are fine as they are."

His face flushed. "I could give you so many more things. A woman with your beauty should have the finer..."

"No, thank you." *I've had it before*.

A muscle twitched near Mr. Every's eye. "There's a charge for me taking care of bugs for you. Maybe you need to clean your apartment. I haven't had complaints from the other tenants."

"A charge? Clean my apartment? Fumigating should be one of your duties as apartment manager." Alex yelped, and Jo loosened her hold on his hand. She mouthed "sorry" and turned back to the scowling man.

"That's the way of it, unless we could come to an agreement of some sort." He leered at her.

"So, unless I give you special privileges, you won't take care of my problem. Is that right?"

"Pretty much." He spit on the floor at her feet.

Jo spun and dragged Alex with her. "Fine. I'll take care of it myself."

She stomped up the stairs, jerking her son along

beside her. "I'm sorry, sweetheart. I've got to get away from that man before I do something bad." Her voice shook, and tears prickled behind her eyelids.

"Are you going to cry, Mommy? Sometimes crying helps." Her son patted her arm.

She blinked back the tears and gave him a shaky smile. "How did you get so smart?"

"I'll kill the bugs for you," Alex said. "Smash them and throw them out the window."

Jo laughed. "There're way too many. And the window is painted shut."

"I can kill some of them. I'll toss them in the garbage. That's better than nothing. Mrs. Leonard stepped on one today. I hardly never see them in her place."

"It's hardly ever, and I'm sure you don't see bugs any where near her. They wouldn't dare." She opened their apartment door and tousled the boy's hair as she let him precede her. "Why don't you go on a bug hunt while I fix us something for dinner?"

She had a difficult time preparing chicken noodle soup and sandwiches as Alex flicked the light on and off in his hunt for the distasteful bugs. She laughed when he yelled triumphantly each time his shoe made contact.

He ran into the kitchen, shoe held high as he chased one of the insects. Jo jumped and shrank back against the wall, cringing at the crunch of the shoe on the bug's armor.

She waited for the light to come back on before

setting the bowls on the small, scarred dining table. The wooden top had once been varnished a honey oak color. Now it was faded. Two plastic lawn chairs served as their seats.

She looked around the room they'd lived in for the past few months. At the faded, peeling, striped wallpaper. She didn't have a clue what its original color had been, but now it was different shades of grey. She took in the chipped paint on the metal kitchen cabinets--the hot plate that served as their stove.

Her son happily ate the meager dinner she'd prepared and the tears threatened again. They lived on soup and sandwiches or macaroni and cheese. Once in a while she'd bring home something from work. A real treat.

Alex was smaller than most of the children in his class. Life should have been different. It *had* been different until she'd married *him*. Not perfect, but not this either. She shook her head, shying from the memory. As if by thinking about him, she would alert him to their presence.

Jo lifted the spoon to her mouth and smiled around the utensil at her son. Alex beamed back at her, and suddenly, the glamorous life she'd lived before her son's birth didn't seem so important.

She sighed and finished her meal then removed the dinner dishes from the table. "Brush your teeth and get in bed. I'll be there in a minute."

The rhythmic movement of her hands as she washed dishes, and the lavender scent of the dish soap soothed her, erasing the fear and stress of the day.

Alex spit into the sink beside her, and she frowned. They couldn't even afford an apartment with a separate bathroom and even with rent as cheap as she paid, she didn't see improvements in the near future. It was like living in the 1900s. What kind of people spit into their kitchen sink? *People in our circumstances, that's who*. She replaced the dishes on the shelf that served as their dish cabinet and turned to usher Alex into bed.

She tucked him into the single bed in the small eight-by-ten foot bedroom and smoothed the dark hair back from his forehead. "You need a haircut." Jo planted a kiss on his forehead. "I'm off work tomorrow. How would you like to play hooky from school?"

"Can we go to the zoo?" A look of hopefulness, mixed with the fear of disappointment, shadowed his face.

Jo wracked her brain for ways of cutting costs in order to be able to afford the outing. They'd manage. Somehow. Alex had too little fun in his life. "You bet."

"Night, Mommy." Alex closed his eyes and turned on his side.

"Goodnight, sweetheart." Jo gave him another glance before closing the door. Her heart lay heavy in her chest as she prepared her bed on the lumpy sofa.

She thought again of her husband, his hard-handed, controlling ways, and punched her pillow into a shape for her head. *God, where are you*?

She sniffed and lay on her back to shift her

weight on broken springs. *I've run for three years. Hoping...praying for a place to raise my son in safety.* A place where his father's long arm and wealth couldn't reach them. *Help us. Please, God.*

*

After the crying woman bolted into the apartment building, Conley headed back the way the woman had come. H stopped in front of the dark alley and listened then ventured toward the opposite end.

Nothing moved. No cat or rat. No dogs howled. A gust of wind rattled the pages of a newspaper, and he swung his head around. Not seeing anyone, he continued his search. Here is where she'd hidden behind the dumpster. A few more feet and he found the torn garbage bags where she'd fallen.

Laughter rang out from the street. He ducked into an alcove.

A man, staggering drunk, and his female companion entered the alley, tottering and giggling. They kissed and groped each other as they fell to the ground, unmindful of the filth and wet.

Conley stuffed his hands into the pockets of his jeans and leaned back, bracing his right leg against the brick wall. He'd acted on a hunch anyway. He doubted she'd be carrying a clue to her real identity.

Ten minutes later, the drunken pair left the alley, leaning on each other for support. The woman laughed shrilly after she tripped and almost fell.

With one last glance around, Conley headed back toward the apartment building. His cowboy boots clomped against the almost deserted street.

He watched the light flicker on in the third floor apartment. The shape of a woman passed by the window. A child's form joined hers, and the woman pulled the child close for a hug. The picture warmed him, despite the chill in the air. He'd been hired to do a job, he no longer had the heart for.

Forty-five minutes later, the apartment light turned off. Conley pushed the button on his watch, illuminating the face. Ten o'clock. He leaned against the wall under a large oak tree and continued to watch the window. His neck ached from peering upward. He waited an hour to see whether the light would come back on. It didn't.

The wind blew colder, and he shoved his hands into the pockets of his jeans, hunching forward. Too bad he hadn't brought a jacket. Long strides carried him quickly down the street. How would he tell the woman who he really was without her running again?

2

Jo gasped for breath. Fear cemented her bronchial tubes together and cut off her oxygen supply. She swiped at her face, flinging multi-legged creatures to the ground. Her mouth opened in a scream, and she spat out the insect which had crawled inside. She gagged. Tremors ran through her.

She slapped at her hair and dislodged whatever creature had chosen to set up residence on her head. She flung her long hair forward and back then scrubbed her scalp with furious hands. Whimpers emanated from her throat.

Her breath wheezed shrilly. The warning sign of an asthma attack. She turned and fell against the wall. She shrieked as the wall moved in waves under her.

Lunging forward, she fell to her hands and knees, not able to see, only to feel the hard armor and prickly legs of many different species of insects and spiders. Some crunched beneath her, others skittered over her fingers. More fell from the darkness above and landed on her head. Her scream reverberated and echoed down the tunnel she suddenly found herself in. A tunnel that spun around her in kaleidoscope colors.

Her chest tightened more…

"Mommy?"

Jo opened her eyes and looked into the worried brown eyes of her son.

"You're having a bad dream, Mommy."

She blinked. Entangled in her blankets, she bolted upright. Beads of perspiration dotted her upper lip. The sheet under her was damp. She couldn't move her legs, and discovered they were lodged under the sofa's arm rest. Pulling herself free, she looked around the sofa and floor until she located her pillow. Throwing aside her coverings, she sat up.

"I'm sorry I woke you, baby. I didn't know I screamed out loud." She placed her head in her hands.

Alex clutched her inhaler. "Do you want to sleep with me? It always helps me to sleep with you when I have a bad dream."

Jo removed her hands and smiled at Alex. "I would love to sleep beside you. It'll keep the bad dreams away."

Her son's smile lit up the dim room as warmth surged through her heart. He handed her the inhaler then grabbed her hand and pulled her behind him. Alex leaped on his bed and bounced. The cheap mattress springs squeaked in protest. "Come on, Mommy."

A slow smile spread across Jo's face, and she crawled in beside him, drawing the quilt over them. The twin bed didn't allow much room for her to stretch. She slid her arm under her son's head. "Well, this is cozy," she told him.

Alex nestled closer. "It's great. What were you dreaming about?"

"Bugs. Lots and lots of bugs." Her skin crawled. She raised the inhaler to her mouth and squeezed, breathing in the bitter vapor.

"I like bugs," Alex said. His voice lowered into a drowsy drawl.

"I don't." Jo hugged him tighter to her as her bronchial tubes opened.

She'd had the same dream several times. What does it mean? She couldn't remember ever having been trapped in a dark place with bugs. She shivered and pulled the blankets closer to her chin. Maybe it was seeing the cockroaches when she turned on the light.

She sighed and gently pulled her arm free, then glanced at her watch. Three-thirty. Jo sighed again and stared at the ceiling. Red and pink lights from a neon sign flashed above her. The bar across the street still seemed to be doing a rousing business.

A door slammed, and a woman giggled. A man cursed. A glass bottle shattered. Someone screamed. *I've got to get Alex out of here. This is no place to raise a child. How much money do I have stashed away? Is it enough?* A tear worked its way down her cheek. She groaned and flopped to her side.

17

*

Alex breathed in Jo's face. "Is it time to get up?"

Jo plopped the pillow over her eyes. "What time is it?"

"Six, three, zero."

Rolling over, Jo groaned then smacked the bed with the palms of her hands. "The zoo doesn't open for two more hours."

"I'm hungry, and we have to catch the bus."

Jo opened one eye and peered at her son. "Thirty more minutes."

"Mom."

She rolled out of bed and frowned. "Fine. What do you want for breakfast?"

"Pancakes."

"Okay, cereal it is."

"You asked me." He frowned.

"I was teasing. You know we only have cereal." Jo smoothed her hair back with her fingers and slipped her feet into worn, pink, terry cloth slippers. "I'm tired, Alex. It's my day off. Go easy on me." She rose from the bed, wrapping the top blanket around her shoulders. "Let's get your cereal and I'll go try to grab a shower."

Alex ran ahead of her, grabbed a bowl of sweetened corn chunks, and added milk. He waved at his mother as she opened the door. She gave him a tired smile, grabbed their basket of bath supplies and terry robe then locked the door behind her.

Still wrapped in the worn blanket, robe slung over her shoulder, she made her way down the hall to the bathroom which serviced those living on the third floor. She breathed a sigh of relief to discover its availability.

She had to lift the door a little and wiggle the latch to get it to slide and lock. She stuck out her bottom lip and exhaled to blow a stray lock of hair out of her face.

She folded the blanket and set it on the closed toilet lid. Gross. Mold and mildew decorated the salmon colored tiles of the bathroom. The shower door was covered with hard water deposits, making visibility through the glass almost impossible.

Jo deposited four quarters into the allotted slots. Careful not to touch the walls or lean against the shower doors, she turned on the faucet and closed the glass door. She hissed as the water sprayed too cold then adjusted to a more comfortable temperature. She stood, letting the water run over her head and through her hair.

Her head bowed, her shoulders slumped, she rested her forehead against the tiles and closed her eyes. She banged her head not too gently against the shower wall. With a huge sigh, getting water in her nose, she straightened and reached for the bottle sitting next to her.

She squirted shampoo in her hand and quickly lathered her hair. Last time she'd showered, the water had shut off and she'd had to deposit more quarters in order to rinse her hair. Quarters she could ill afford to spend.

Five minutes later, she stepped out, toweled dry, then slipped into the thread bare terry robe she'd brought with her. She fought with the latch on the door again, slammed the door open, and ran into the paunch of Mr. Every.

"What a pleasant surprise."

"Mr. Every." She nodded and moved to step past him.

His arm shot out and trapped her between the door and him. "Been thinking about my proposition yesterday?"

"Not really." Jo tried to sidle past him.

Mr. Every stepped sideways, keeping her in front of him. "Life could be easier...and more pleasant." He wiggled his eyebrows. "For both of us."

"For you, maybe." Jo ducked and escaped. She scurried back to her apartment. She stopped at the door and turned. Mr. Every watched her. She pushed the door open and rushed inside.

"Who's ready to go to the zoo?" she asked.

Alex jumped up. "Me."

"Let me get dressed, and we'll be off." Jo ruffled her son's hair and ducked into the privacy of the bedroom.

She dressed in faded blue jeans, a long sleeved red tee-shirt and tennis shoes. She tossed a lightweight denim jacket over her shoulders and grabbed a sweatshirt for Alex.

Mr. Every poked his head out of his apartment as Jo and Alex clambered down the stairs. The boy stuck his tongue out at the landlord. "Stop it." Jo chuckled in spite of herself.

She grabbed her son's hand, and they stepped into a sunny, cool day. Jo's spirits lifted. A large oak tree shaded the apartment complex, and warbling birds perched on its branches. She could almost believe they were like normal people.

Jo smiled at people she passed and linked her hand with Alex's to swing their arms. Her steps were light as they headed down the sidewalk. One man stood on a street corner. He looked vaguely familiar to her, and she glanced twice before continuing across the street. He smiled and waved. Her smile wavered as she returned the gesture.

Two streets over, Jo and Alex caught the bus to the city zoo.

Alex knelt on the seat, looking behind him while Jo stared out the window. The man stood on the sidewalk and watched the bus pass. Her brows drew together. Where had she seen him before? At work. He was the new bus boy.

She drew in a sharp breath. And last night. He'd tried to stop her and asked if she needed help. Turning her head away from the window, Jo sat back against the seat.

Alex bumped her shoulder, and she pulled him down beside her. "Sit still."

"I'm looking at that man. He smiled at me."

Jo whirled in her seat, heart thudding against her rib cage. "What man?"

Alex pointed and lurched forward when the bus stopped. A crowd of people surged forward, and Jo strained to see the man her son had pointed out. She caught a glimpse of dark hair before the man disappeared down the bus steps. The bus boy had lighter colored hair. Who was this man?

Jo half-stood and stretched her neck to see out the opposite windows. With a shake of her head, she sat back down. She was paranoid. She was sure the man was just what he seemed. A bored passenger amusing himself with a child.

A half-hour later, the bus halted at the entrance to the zoo. Jo reclaimed her son's hand to keep him close as she navigated the crowd on the sidewalk. "Ready?" She smiled at him.

"Ready." Alex skipped with excitement.

Jo dug the money from the pocket of her jeans and purchased their tickets.

"I want to see the monkeys first," Alex said.

"Don't you want to follow the map?" Jo asked as he pulled her along in his wake. "We don't want to miss anything."

"Later." He let go of Jo's hand and ducked under the rope that separated the walkway from the enclosure. Alex pressed against the wires of the cage. Monkeys squealed and darted.

"Get back." Jo pulled her son across the rope. "Stay behind this barrier. Understand?"

She looked up, and her eyes locked with the busboy from work. Her mouth fell open in surprise, then clamped shut. Was he following them? He'd been outside their apartment yesterday, on the sidewalk when the bus pulled away...and now here at the zoo.

The man smiled and continued down the path away from them. Jo grabbed Alex's hand. "Let's go."

"Where? I'm not finished watching the monkeys." Alex continued to protest as his mother dragged him.

"Let's go to the reptile house. You like snakes and lizards." She shoved her hip against the door and cast glances to each side of the building then entered the dim recesses. The reptile house was home to almost a hundred different species of snakes. A group of children dressed in royal blue tee shirts pressed against the glass exhibits.

Alex ran ahead to ooh and aah over a mighty python. Jo leaned against the cool block wall and wiped sweat from her brow. A sliver of light cut through the gloom as someone entered the building.

Jo waited for the person to turn the corner into the aisle where she stood. The footsteps stopped. A distorted shadow fell past the wall.

Fear knotted her stomach, and she pushed Alex on to the next exhibit. The footsteps continued. Jo whipped around. The figure of a man ducked around the corner.

She urged Alex on and tossed furtive glances over her shoulder but didn't see the man again. Another cast of light, and an alarm sounded, signaling someone using the fire escape door.

She turned to watch her son push a button, illuminating a nocturnal exhibit. "Just push it once. You'll make the animals dizzy."

"They're not animals. They're reptiles." When he'd finished, Alex shoved the exit door open with enough force to send someone crashing into the bushes next to the reptile building.

Jo pulled Alex close to her and turned. She glanced back. The man from her job got to his feet and brushed himself off.

"Stay here," she ordered Alex.

She marched up to the man and poked him in the chest with her index finger. She put her hands on her hips. "Who are you, and why do you keep following us?'

"I'm not following you." The man tucked his shirt into his jeans.

"Yes, you are. What's your name? Conrad something?"

He sighed. "Conley Hook."

"Why are you following me?"

Conley put his hands up. "I'm not." He waved his hand. "It's a beautiful day. I'm new to town, and thought I'd spend it at the zoo."

Jo narrowed her eyes. "Hmm-hmm."

"Really." He held out a hand to her. "You're Jocelyn. I've seen you at work, but since I just started I don't know anyone."

She stared at the offered hand for a minute. "I go by Jo."

"No last name?"

"Thomas." Jo turned to go.

"Wait. Since you're here, and I'm here…"

"No." She took Alex's hand and walked away.

"I'll buy the two of you an ice cream."

Alex's eyes brightened, and his dark gaze darted from Jo's face to Conley's. Jo sighed and gave in to the inevitable. An ice cream at the zoo was a rare treat, one she couldn't afford to give her son. "All right. Just an ice cream and then, we go our *separate* ways." She gave her son a stern look, took a firm grasp of his upper arm, and led him to a picnic bench. "Be good," she whispered. She wiped the seat with a napkin before sitting down.

Within minutes, Conley returned and handed them each a vanilla and chocolate swirl ice cream cone. "I didn't ask which you preferred, so I got both."

Jo ran her tongue across the icy creaminess. She closed her eyes and savored the treat. She didn't know Mr. Conley Hook any more than she knew the President, but if he *was* following them, sitting down and enjoying an ice cream would keep things out in the open.

"Why is your arm painted?" Alex asked Conley.

"Alex!" Jo's eyes popped open. She'd noticed the tattoo on Conley's arm. A fabric-draped cross, graced his forearm.

"It's okay." Conley rolled up his sleeve. "I've got a panther head here."

Jo allowed her eyes to travel to his right bicep

and on to Conley's face. Intelligent blue eyes watched her under lashes too dark and long for a man. Dark blond hair covered his head. A curl fell forward to cover one eye.

He brushed the lock away from his face and laughed. "Yeah, I'm pretty. It kind of dispels the tough guy image I try to portray."

Jo snorted and took a big mouthful of her ice cream. His build didn't match the shape of the man in the reptile house. Conley's shoulders were bigger. His legs longer. But she still thought he was following them. Why? She half-listened as he tried to explain to a young child why he had painted pictures on his arms.

"I was bored one day in jail and decided that when I got out, I'd get a tattoo."

"You're a convict?" The ice cream stuck in Jo's throat.

"*Ex*-convict," he was quick to reassure her. "I've been released for a long time."

"Hurry and eat your ice cream, Alex." The thought of eating ice cream with a convict was ludicrous, and she fought the urge laugh.

Conley's hand shot out as she started to rise. "It's okay, really. I was a juvenile in for stealing and racing cars. Nothing violent. That was fifteen years ago. I'm not the same man, or boy, I guess."

Jo studied him. His eyes silently pleaded with her to understand.

"Please," he said. "Stay. Enjoy your ice cream."

"All right." She sat back down. He stared

unblinking at her. Jo fidgeted and looked away to transfer her attention to her son. She patted Alex on his shoulder and nodded. "Go ahead and finish."

Conley stayed by them as they wandered the rest of the zoo. The man joked with Alex and carried him on his shoulders when his little legs showed signs of fatigue. He remained courteous with Jo and laughed when she jumped at a tiger's roar. He cupped her elbow for support when they walked across a rough patch of ground, and he kept her and Alex supplied with cold bottles of water.

Eventually, Jo grew comfortable in his presence. His attention, rather than causing her to feel like a confined prisoner, made her feel special and worthy. The man kept her and Alex laughing with tales of his naughty youth. She smiled and allowed herself the freedom to enjoy the day.

As loud speakers announced the zoo's impending closure, Conley escorted them to the bus stop. She smiled down at him from the top step of the bus. "Thank you for a wonderful day."

"My pleasure." Conley bowed. "Thank *you* for letting me impose."

Jo's gaze remained glued on him as she stepped back into the bus and the doors whooshed closed. She'd spotted two different men today. Just glimpses. Possibly coincidence but she didn't believe in coincidence. Could he have found her? Was it time to uproot Alex again and move? She blinked back tears. Just when maybe, they'd made a friend.

3

Conley bussed the breakfast tables when Jo entered the restaurant the next morning. His muscles rippled beneath the white tee shirt he wore. He smiled a welcome. Heat rose in her face.

She flashed him a half-smile and disappeared into the back where employees were allowed to deposit their personal belongings. "I can't believe I was staring," she muttered. "How embarrassing."

"Hey, Jo Jo!"

Jo turned to greet another waitress. "Hey, Lilly." The other woman wore ruby red lipstick over full lips.

Lilly hung her sweater on a peg and fluffed her bleached, over-processed hair. "Have you seen the new busboy? What a find!"

"Yes. His name is Conley." Jo hung her worn brown sweater next to the other waitress's fluorescent pink one.

"Oooh, you lucky girl," Lilly cooed. "You *have*

met him." She turned. The woman's eyes narrowed and raked over Jo's sweater. She returned her gaze to Jo's face. "Why are you so plain Jane all the time? You're pretty enough if you'd just bother to put a little effort into your appearance." Lilly smoothed a tight white shirt over ample curves. A black straight line skirt hugged a full bottom. A vinyl belt cinched her waist tight.

"What's wrong with the way I look?" Jo peered into the mirror hanging above the coat pegs. She wore a loose white blouse tucked into pleated black slacks. She reached up and tightened her ponytail. "Besides, we weren't talking about me."

"Oh, yeah." Lilly wiggled her fingers. "Come on, tell all."

Jo shrugged. "There really isn't anything to tell." She wished she'd kept her mouth shut.

"The fact you're keeping quiet speaks volumes." Lilly fluffed her hair.

"Actually," Conley came up behind Jo. "We had quite a day yesterday. We went to the zoo and ate ice cream. The two of us and her son." He put his arms around Jo's waist and pulled her close.

Jo's eyes widened and she turned. Her face came in close proximity with his chest. Placing her hands palm flat, she pushed.

Conley winked, and released her. The other woman giggled and slipped from the employee lounge.

"Sorry about that," Conley said, hanging up his apron. "But that woman is a piranha. You looked caught and helpless. I've always wanted to play the role of hero."

"I'm anything but helpless," Jo retorted.

He laughed. "Okay, I'm the helpless one. You saved me from her."

"A lot of men would be pleased with attention from Lilly."

"I prefer my women clean and natural." He winked at her again.

"Keep looking. Maybe you'll find that special someone." She grabbed a clean apron from a shelf near the door and stalked out. His laughter followed. In spite of herself, she smiled. He did seem to have a way of making her feel good about herself.

Business boomed that Saturday. Jo's feet ached, and she forced a smile as she took yet another customer's order. She handed the cook the order slip and folded her arms on the counter. With a sigh, she rested her head on them.

"This must be your week for handsome men," Lilly whispered in her ear. She barked out a menu order and leaned against the corner.

"Why?" Jo asked, not lifting her head.

"Well, there's this really hot, expensive looking dish sitting in my area. Pricey cologne, Armani suit."

Jo raised her head.

"He asked about you," the other woman sang as she turned and walked away, hips swinging.

Jo looked toward the section where Lilly served tables, and observed a man with dark hair exit the restaurant through the side door. Her heart stopped. He had the same build as the man at the zoo. Why would a man with money be interested in her?

Unless...She glanced around the diner. And why would he be eating here? The man looked familiar and it continued to nag at her mind the rest of her shift. At one point, she swore someone watched her, and she whirled around to glimpse a man dart past the restaurant window. She shook her head. *I'm getting paranoid.*

After eight hours on her feet serving customers, and another hour rolling eating utensils inside napkins, Jo was more than ready to head home. She waved to Lilly and pushed the door open to step into a frigid wind. She jumped back as a Harley-Davidson motorcycle roared to a stop beside her.

The driver removed his helmet and gave Jo a lopsided grin. "Want a ride?" Conley asked.

She pulled her sweater tighter around her, and walked away. "No thanks." She hunched over and stumbled headlong into the biting cold.

He swung his leg over and hopped off the bike. "Come on. It's cold out here. We could go get a cup of coffee."

Jo shook her head. "I've got to pick up Alex."

"Riding on my bike will be faster."

She stopped and glared at him. The wind picked up, pulling her hair free of the rubber band and whipping it around her face. With one hand, Jo held her sweater close and with the other, pulled her hair back.

Her gaze clashed with Conley's cobalt blue one. "Why is it so important to you that I be your friend?"

He blinked. "I like you."

"How do you know? We've only just met." She turned and marched away from him. "Go away."

"One cup." He hopped and caught up with her.

The pleading in his voice tugged at her heart. She sighed. "One cup, but I'm not getting on the back of that...thing. It's too dangerous."

"It's not dangerous. It's exhilarating."

"I said no. Now, do you want me to have a cup of coffee with you or not?"

"Okay." He ran back, kicked up the kickstand and pushed the bike alongside her. A huge grin split his face.

She laughed. "You're like Alex. A little boy, nagging his mother for some candy after he's been told he's had enough."

"You're as sweet as candy." His gaze caressed her face.

Her face grew warm despite the cold evening, and she turned away from him.

They didn't speak again until Conley held the coffee shop door open for her. "Your pleasure awaits, mi'lady."

The aroma of hot coffee and warm cinnamon buns hung in the air of the shop. Since she wasn't paying, she decided to splurge and chose a frozen mocha drink with whipped cream. She chose a booth in the back and waited for Conley to join her.

The forest green vinyl creaked beneath her as she settled into a comfortable position. The flecked Formica top shone with a heavy wax. Jo absently shoved the napkin dispenser to watch it slide.

She glanced up and shook her head as Conley smiled and flirted with the young girl behind the counter. She couldn't help but return his smile when he flashed one in her direction. The man definitely oozed charm.

Conley set her frozen coffee before her. "Can't understand why you want a cold coffee when it's freezing outside." He scooted into the booth. He wrapped his hands around his Styrofoam mug and blew into his hot coffee.

Jo wrestled her gaze away from his lips.

"I'll tell you," he said.

Jo sucked on her straw. Sharp pain infused her sinuses, and she pinched the bridge of her nose against the ache. "Tell me what?"

"Why I'm pursuing you." He lifted the paper mug to his nose, and sniffed.

"Pursuing me?" Despite her struggle to control the mounting fear, Jo's voice squeaked.

He unwrapped his hands from around the cup and leaned back. "Well, not really pursuing, but when I saw you the first time, I knew I had to help you. That you were more than just a job to me."

She opened her mouth to reply and stopped. Over Conley's shoulder, she caught a glimpse of a man with dark hair, standing by the door. The man turned, and Jo caught a quick look of his profile. She quickly registered the fact he sported a short beard and moustache. She frowned. If she could only get a look at his face.

"What?" Conley looked over his shoulder.

"That man by the door. I swear I saw him at the zoo yesterday, and I *know* he was at the restaurant today. He asked about me. I feel like I know him, but I can't get a good look at his face. There's something about the way he walks. The way he carries himself."

Conley turned back. "He asked about you?"

"Yes. To Lilly."

"What did she tell him?"

She shrugged. "I don't know. He left."

Conley's entire demeanor changed from carefree to rock-hard serious. He reached across the table and grabbed Jo's hand. "Let's go." He stood and pulled her with him. "You're riding my Harley. No arguments."

"Wait. What's going on? Who is that man?"

He led Jo out the back door and pulled her along so she had to run to keep up with his long stride. Conley plopped the motorcycle helmet on her head. She grimaced as it banged against her skull. Before Jo had time to register the horrifying fact she was on the back of a motorcycle, they roared down the street toward her apartment.

Forgetting modesty, she plastered herself to Conley's back and wrapped her arms around his waist. Shivers took control of her body, and she pressed closer to capture some of his warmth.

She found it difficult to breath with her nose flattened against his back, and she turned her head. The mild vibration of the bike aggravated the beginning of a headache.

The cold wind brought tears to Jo's eyes and made her nose run. She sniffed. The city buildings zipped past them. The growl of the Harley drowned out the city sounds. Conley veered the bike sharply to the right, around a parked car and a small shriek escaped Jo. She tightened her grip. *God, help me. What am I doing on this death trap?*

When they screeched to a halt outside her building, Conley helped her from the bike and deposited her on shaky legs.

"Th...thank you, I think." Jo handed him the helmet.

Conley nodded. "I'll stay here until you're safely inside."

"There's no need." She stepped back and studied him. His gaze stayed glued on her face, his full lips set into a firm line. The blond curls were tangled and tousled from the windy ride.

"What happened back there?" she asked.

He put the helmet on his head and fastened the strap beneath his chin. "What?"

"Do you know the man in the coffee shop?"

Conley averted his eyes. "No. I've never met him."

"Let me be more specific. Do you know *who* he

is?"

Exhaling sharply, he removed the helmet. "Let's get your son, and then we'll talk."

"We'll talk now."

Conley steered her into the building. "After we get Alex." He kept her arm firmly in his grasp as they climbed the stairs.

Mr. Every met them on his way down. He opened his mouth to say something, took one look at Conley's face, and promptly clamped his lips closed. Jo tossed an anxious glance over her shoulder as they left the apartment manager staring after them.

She tried to pull her arm free from Conley's grip. "You're going too fast. Conley, stop. You're hurting me."

"Sorry." He didn't loosen his grip until they stopped before Mrs. Leonard's door.

Jo glanced up at him. "How do you know where my babysitter lives?"

Ignoring her, Conley banged on the door. Once it opened, he shoved Jo inside and closed the door behind them.

"Excuse me," Mrs. Leonard said, taking a step back. "You leave my apartment this instant. I don't know who you are. You have no right to barge in here…"

"As soon as we have Alex." Conley glanced around the room. "Where is he?"

"The restroom."

"You let him go to the restroom alone?" Jo

whipped the door open and sprinted down the hall, Conley close on her heels. She tried the restroom door and found it locked.

"Alex?" Jo knocked on the door. "It's Mommy. Let me in." There was no answer.

Conley stepped back and delivered a powerful kick which sent the door crashing open. The small room was empty.

"Alex?" Jo whirled. "Where is he? Alex?" She stepped back into the hall. By this time, several of the tenants stared into the hall. Tears welled in Jo's eyes. Her heart pounded a fierce rhythm in her chest. "Conley?"

"Stay here." He bounded down the stairs. His footsteps echoed through the stairwell. Within moments he returned, grabbed Jo's arm again and pulled her up the stairs to the third floor. He stepped aside while she unlocked her apartment with trembling hands.

Rushing into the room ahead of her, Conley pulled a revolver from beneath his shirt and searched the room. His gaze roamed across the small space.

"You've got a gun?" Jo stood in the middle of the room. Her hands hung limp at her sides. A cold fist grabbed her intestines and squeezed. The room spun around her. "Who are you? Where's my son?" Her voice lowered to a whisper. "How do you know so much about us?"

He reached behind her and shut the door. Taking her hand more gently than he'd grabbed her arm earlier, he led her to the sofa and pushed her down onto it. He grabbed one of the kitchen chairs, placed it in front of her, and straddled it.

"Five years ago, you left, and divorced, your husband, Nielson Blake." He held up a hand to stop her as she opened her mouth to interrupt. "You disappeared, leaving only a note addressed to your parents. Blake went berserk. He searched everywhere for you, not caring who got hurt in the process. Your nanny was killed."

Jo choked and put a hand to her mouth. Tears welled in her eyes and spilled over.

"A year ago you made the mistake of contacting your parents by phone, then mailed them a postcard, correct?"

Jo nodded. "But I mailed it from a different city. I've moved so many times." She sniffed.

Conley reached across to the table and grabbed a box of tissues to hand to her. "Your parent's home was broken into. They didn't think anything had been taken, but they were mistaken. Blake found the postcard. He's been tracking you ever since. A couple of months after the break-in, your mother discovered the card missing. She contacted me. My name is Conley Hook. I'm a private investigator hired by your parents to locate and protect you."

Her eyes never left Conley's face. Suddenly the features of the man following her fell into place. "The man who's been following me is Blake. He's let his hair grow and he grew a beard." She shook her head in disbelief. "He's changed. I didn't recognize him."

Conley leaned forward and took her hand in his. "He hasn't changed that much. Not really. I believe he now has your son, Alex. He is *your* son, right? Not Blake's?"

She nodded. "I was pregnant when I married Blake. He said it didn't matter. That he loved me enough to love some other man's child. He was delighted when I had a boy." Her eyes grew wide. She lowered her voice. Tremors shook her body. "He sells children, Conley. To the highest bidder. That's how he makes his money. I thought he would kill me when I found out." All the fear and horror of her discovery threatened to choke her. To chill her blood to the point it no longer ran through her veins. Oh, what were they going to do now?

He squeezed her hand and let go. "I know. We'll find him."

"My parents hired you." Jo still couldn't believe what was happening. Her thoughts spun in circles, making her dizzy. She leaned forward and rested her head on her knees. "How did you find me?"

He smiled. "It took a year. You're good. I looked in every town close to the postmark on your card. I looked in every minimum wage job in those towns. I found you a week ago and obtained a job in the same restaurant." He leaned closer to her. "Blake found you, too. It only took him a week longer than it did me."

She jumped up and leaned against the kitchen corner. "Why didn't you tell me who you were?"

"Your parents just wanted me to watch you. They wanted to know you were all right."

She shook her head. "No, they want you to bring me back. Right?"

"Yes."

"Well. Here I am." She held out her hands. "Take me back. Blake has Alex. He'll take him back to Prestige. Now *you* take me."

"I can't," Conley explained. A muscle quivered at his jaw. "Not after I found out what kind of man Blake really is."

Jo kicked the leg of the table. She screamed as loud as she could. The force of it hurt her throat. A neighbor banged on the thin wall and shouted for her to shut up.

Conley leaped to his feet and pulled her into his arms. He held her tight as her screams faded to sobs. He continued to hold her as the sobs turned to hiccups, and the hiccups to a whispered prayer.

"You've got to take me to my son," she gasped. "I don't care about the danger. If we don't go back, Alex will be sold. I never should have married Blake, but I believed him! I believed he would love Alex as his own.

"I'll take you." He stroked her hair. "But you have to let me protect you."

4

Alex squeaked as the man burst through the bathroom door, clapped a hand over his mouth, and flung the boy over his shoulder. The door banged closed behind them.

Biting as hard as he could on the fleshy part of the man's palm, he tasted blood and pulled his head free as the man cursed. A sharp slap and Alex cried.

The boy's shrieks echoed through the hall. "Shut up!" The man shook the child, sending the boy into a fresh wave of screams.

No heads poked from apartment doorways as the man and boy clattered down the stairway. Blaring televisions sounded through closed doors. A baby wailed. Just as they disappeared through the front doors of the building, Alex heard his mother scream his name.

"Mommy!"

His captor yanked the car door open and shoved Alex inside. The boy's head collided with the door frame and colored spots danced before his eyes. The door slammed. He lifted his head as his captor slid behind the wheel. The car roared to life and raced down the street.

Alex's screams subsided into sobs and he curled into a ball on the back seat.

"Mommy," he whispered.

"Stop your blubbering, kid. You're going to see your dad."

"My dad?" Alex wiped the back of his hand across his face and got to his knees. "Mommy told me my daddy was dead."

"Don't believe everything your mother tells you, kid." The car swerved sharply. Alex crashed into the door. "Put your seatbelt on."

Alex scrambled for the belt as the car careened around another corner and he landed on the floor. Scurrying back onto the seat, he grabbed the seatbelt and stretched it across the front of him, sliding it into the clasp. "Will my mommy be there?"

"I doubt it."

The car screeched to a halt and the door next to Alex was wrenched open. The man once again flung the boy over his shoulder and strode quickly to a motel room door. He rapped on the door, fidgeting from foot to foot until it opened.

He walked inside and tossed Alex onto the bed. "Here's your kid. Where's my money?"

"Here. One thousand dollars. As agreed."

Alex sat quietly as the first man left the room. The boy scooted back against the bed's headboard as the other man stood and stared down at him.

*

"Hello, Alex. I'm your father." Blake sat on the edge of the bed, next to the frightened boy. "Has your mother told you about me?"

Alex shook his head. "She said you were dead."

The man laughed. "As you can see, I am very much alive." He stood and paced the room. "Tomorrow, I will take you home. Eventually your mother will join us. We'll be together again. As a family." *How can she resist? I have her son.*

"Mommy's coming?"

The man stopped pacing and stood beside the bed. "Yes, Mommy's coming." Blake pulled down the bedcovers. "Slide in. We'll leave in the morning."

"Mommy always reads to me."

"We'll have to skip this one night. I don't have any books with me."

"She prays with me too."

"I don't pray." Blake pulled the covers beneath Alex's chin. "Now go to sleep."

"I'm thirsty."

"Go to sleep!"

Alex cowered beneath the blankets. "But I always use the restroom before I go to bed."

Blake yanked the covers down, pulled the boy from the bed, and shoved him toward the bathroom.

"Make it quick. You're stalling."

Once he'd gotten the boy into bed and quiet, Blake stripped down to his designer silk boxers and crawled beneath the blankets of the other single bed. He grimaced as the low thread-count sheets rasped against his skin. Used to the comfort of Egyptian cotton, his skin crawled.

He focused on revenge once he had Jocelyn in his clutches. He smiled at his cleverness in believing he'd divorced her on grounds of abandonment. How dare she divorce him? He'd almost thought of refusing, but then realized how it could play into his plan.

Now, her parents sympathized with his plight. He'd played the grieving, abused husband well. A laugh escaped him at the thought of them hiring a private investigator.

Having his own people watch Jocelyn's parents, thus learning of the investigator, had landed their daughter right back where he wanted her. Blake never willingly relinquished control of any possession. The night passed, the light grew dim, and Blake's eyes closed to the sound of light snores emanating from the boy.

Bright morning light through the threadbare curtains woke him, and Blake rolled over to see the boy staring at him. "Yes?"

"You sleep late."

"Your point?" Blake slid his legs over the side of the mattress and ran both hands through his hair.

"We always get up early. I have to go to school,

and Mommy goes to work. She sometimes works at night, too."

"Work is for the poor. I have no need for it."

Alex's eyes grew larger. "You mean we're rich?"

"No, I mean *I'm* rich." He stood and popped the kinks from his back. He grabbed the pants he'd laid over an armchair and got dressed. The bastard kid would never see a dime of Blake's money.

"What's for breakfast?" The boy slid from the bed and stood in front of him.

"What would you like?" Blake retrieved his wallet and keys from the nightstand and put them in his pocket.

"McDonalds."

"Fine." Blake frowned. "Your mother allowed you to eat fast food?"

"Not much."

"This is a treat, right?"

"Right!"

Blake held the door open for the boy then scanned the room for anything he might have forgotten. He saw nothing and tossed the motel room keys on the bureau and closed the door.

"Get in the back," he barked as Alex went to slide into the front passenger seat. The boy's face fell.

"And no talking. I don't like talking in the mornings." Blake slid the key into the ignition of the silver Mercedes. "And I really don't want to drive across country listening to the nonsensical babblings of a child." The boy's sobs drifted over the front seat. "And

quit that squalling or I won't be stopping at
McDonald's."

Horrified he actually might be seen patronizing
the fast food restaurant, Blake pulled behind the
building. No one here should know him, but a man of
his reputation couldn't be too careful.

He clenched his jaw upon realizing he'd have to
stand in line to place his order. The drive-through lane
already held several cars. Inside, ten people stood
before him and he glanced repeatedly at his Rolex.
"Finally." He turned to Alex. "What do you want?"

"I'm having breakfast with my dad," the boy
stated. "And I want pancakes."

Blake repeated the boy's order and added a cup
of coffee. When Alex moved to sit in one of the vinyl
booths, the man shook his head. "Eat in the car...and if
you spill one drop, I'll make you sorry."

He tipped the cup to his lips and spit it out.
"Awful stuff." He tossed the cup to the ground and
pressed the lock release on the car's fob.

"That's littering."

Blake held the door open for the boy and
slammed it closed behind him. "You're a sassy boy,
aren't you?"

"Mommy told me never to litter."

Blake sighed. The smell of the sweet pancakes
made him nauseous and increased his ill-temper. The
car's tires squealed as he raced from the parking lot. He
accelerated and sped to the nearby access road and
onto the freeway.

"Uh oh," Alex's whisper reached Blake's ears.

"Did you spill?" The man swerved the car to the shoulder of the road. "Tell me you didn't spill." He cut off the ignition and strode to the back door. Heat rose into his face as he surveyed the damage.

Pancakes and syrup ran down the boy's legs and onto the leather seats. Blake cursed and pulled Alex from the car, throwing the boy to the ground. "I told you not to spill anything. Didn't I?" He towered over Alex and kicked up the dirt. "Do you know how much that car cost me? Do you care?"

"Is there a problem here?"

Blake swerved to see a police officer swing a leg off a motorcycle and remove his helmet.

"Now look what you've done," he hissed at the boy. "Get up and don't say a word."

"Were you about to strike that boy?"

"No, sir. He's feeling ill and we had to pull over, right son?"

Alex nodded. Blake held out a hand and helped the boy to his feet. "He's much better now."

The officer looked toward the car. "May I see your vehicle registration and your driver's license, please?"

"Why? Is there a problem?" Blake squeezed the boy's hand.

"Just procedure."

Blake nodded and pulled Alex along with him. Bending low to the boy's ear, he whispered, "Get in the car and don't talk. Understand?"

Alex nodded.

Blake opened the door and pulled down the glove box to withdraw the requested papers. A small, 50-caliber, antique derringer with a pearl handle lay nestled beneath them. He retrieved the gun and stuck it in the pocket of his pants.

"Here they are." He handed them to the officer. "Everything should be in order."

The officer perused the papers and handed them back. "Where y'all headed?"

"Back home. My son and I are just driving across country. Taking in the sights."

"Have a safe trip." The officer turned and walked back to his bike. He nodded a goodbye before donning his helmet and driving back onto the freeway.

Blake squared his shoulders. He glanced to the car where Alex waited.

5

Conley stared at Jo's sleeping face. Her dark lashes cast shadows on her pale cheeks. He rubbed his chin. His hand rasped against the day-old whiskers.

He ached to run his fingers through the long auburn strands, shot with gold that fanned over her pillow like dark fire. Clutched in her hand, Jo held her son's pajama top. What started as just another job for Conley had turned into something more personal.

He remembered the first time he'd spotted Jo in person. He could recall everything about that day, as if a movie replayed the events inside his head. She'd been waiting on tables at the restaurant, oblivious to everyone around her but the customer. She had a way of making each person feel as if they were the only one in the restaurant. Her hair had been drawn back into a ponytail. A tired smile pasted on her face. She'd looked at the clock hanging behind the counter on her way to the kitchen.

Conley had glanced down at the photograph her mother gave him and compared the laughing young woman in the picture to the tense and anxious one standing in front of him. His heart skipped a beat as she'd turned in his direction, looking at him, yet not really seeing him. He'd thought her the most beautiful woman he'd ever seen.

He sat on the edge of the small bed where he'd deposited her last night. She'd cried herself to sleep in his arms, railing against the injustice of her ex-husband and her fear over what he would do to Alex.

Leaning forward and balancing his elbows on his thighs, Conley put his head in his hands and scratched his head.

"Your hair is sticking up in all directions."

Conley lifted his head to see Jo looking at him.

"I need to call my parents." She sat up and flung off the blanket. "They need to be on the look-out for Blake."

"Okay." Conley stood and held out a hand to help her. "Pack a small bag. We'll be riding the Harley."

"Are you serious? We have five states to go through." Jo's eyes widened.

"Do you have another means of transportation, because I don't?" Conley tossed her one of the saddlebags from his bike. "Take only what will fit in here." He took a couple of steps toward the door before turning. "Oh, and pack a dress. We'll be stopping in Vegas to get married. We'll be there by nightfall."

"Married!" Jo's voice squeaked. "I'm not going

to marry you. You're crazy. You've got a lot of nerve. I don't even know you."

"We'll be traveling and living very closely with each other. It'll be better if we're married. We'll be better equipped to battle Blake over custody of Alex if you're married."

She popped her head through the door. "Alex isn't his. He doesn't have any rights to him."

"Tell your ex-husband that. His wallet can speak volumes. We don't have to stay married. An annulment will be easy enough to get."

Her head disappeared through the doorway and something hit the wall. A picture fell. She reappeared in the doorway of the bedroom and threw the saddle bag at him. "Don't expect any rights."

He caught the saddlebag. "I won't. It'll be name only. Once we're married, we'll post an announcement in your hometown paper and mention the fact your son is missing, presumably kidnapped by your ex-husband." He grinned. "How's that for stirring things up?"

"I like it, except for the getting married part."

Man, she's cute. He reached over and opened the door. "After you." He winked as she stalked by.

She tossed her head and stomped down the stairs ahead of him.

They stopped in front of the manager's apartment, and Conley rapped on the door.

"What?" A sleepy Evers opened the door.

Conley handed the disgruntled man a hundred dollar bill. "Pack up Ms. Thomas's things and store them. She'll be back for them in a few weeks. We're getting married." He patted Evers on his protruding stomach. "That's a good man."

"I told him my name was Kingsley," Jo said.

Evers looked like a fish out of water. His mouth opened and closed as Conley ushered Jo out of the building. He cast a glance over his shoulder. Evers still stared after them as they stashed Jo's saddlebag on the back of the Harley.

Conley handed her the helmet and mounted the bike. He gave the man a wave and patted the hand which settled against his hip. He pulled Jo tighter to him, enjoying the feel of her against his back, and they sped away.

They exited onto the freeway and merged swiftly with the busy morning traffic. Two miles down the interstate, Jo shuddered. He could tell from her trembles that she cried.

He chose the next off-ramp and stopped in the shade of a large tree. Slinging his leg around, he pulled Jo onto his lap and removed her helmet. Once again he held her as she cried herself dry.

*

Holding tight around Conley's waist, the trembling overcame Jo when they reached the interstate. With nothing to occupy her thoughts but the scenery flashing by, the tears had started. Slowly at first, then building into a full scale sob fest.

She shook her head, blubbering and protesting as Conley drew her into his lap. He smoothed her hair, and she gave into his tenderness.

"How did you meet Blake?"

She jerked her head up and stared into Conley's face. "What?"

"Blake. How did you meet him?"

"Um...I was a coffee barrista."

"Go on." Conley situated them more firmly on the bike's seat.

"I was flattered by his attentions. He came in every morning for a cup of coffee and insisted I be the one to serve him." It wasn't until later that she'd discovered his primary attraction to her was because she was so obviously untrained in most cultural manners. She'd been clay to be molded in his hands.

"Blake wanted a trophy wife. Someone he could put on display. He told me how to dress, how to wear my hair." She laughed and put a hand to her untamed curls. "He hated my curls. He drilled me before every social event, making sure I knew exactly how to act."

"And if you failed?"

Jo scooted off the bike. "Then I paid for it." She ground the words out between her teeth.

"How?"

"I don't want to talk about it." She stepped away, turning to face down the freeway, arms folded tight across her chest. Images of being locked in a room until bruises could be hidden flooded through her mind. Jo shook as fearful thoughts of not finding Alex in time flowed through her.

"Shhh," Conley walked up and rubbed her back.

He pulled her into him as if she were an infant. "We'll find him. I promise."

"That's a promise you might not be able to keep." Her words were muffled by his chest.

"I'll keep it." His arms tightened. "Just get it out. We'll wait."

"Don't patronize me." Jo rubbed her face on his shirt then raised her head. "I'm ready. We shouldn't waste anymore time. Blake's only getting farther ahead of us."

Conley stared into her face. "Okay. Get your helmet back on and lower the face plate."

"Face plate?"

He tapped the helmet and showed her how to flip down the face plate. "So I don't get so wet." Sniffing, Jo placed the helmet on her head.

"Let me know if we need to stop again."

"I won't need to."

He bumped her. "Anxious to get to Vegas?"

Jo scowled as he pushed her into the motorcycle, and she banged her side. "Right. That's it."

She climbed on behind him after Conley mounted. Leaning back, she tapped his shoulder, signaling she was ready. With a roar, they sped back to the interstate.

A lump caught in her throat, and she leaned her head forward, the helmet resting between Conley's shoulder blades. *What if Blake doesn't go to Prestige? I need to call my parents. I'll have to do that when we reach Vegas. Vegas? What am I doing?*

She tapped on his back again, then waited until he pulled to the side of the road. "What?" His bright eyes narrowed.

"Are you sure we can get an annulment?"

"That's why we're going to Vegas. I'll say I was drunk or something. Trust me. Is this why we stopped?"

She nodded. "I couldn't speak to you while we were zooming down the road. What if we got into an accident?"

"You beat all. Vegas is two hours away. Do you think we can drive that long without stopping again?"

Jo nodded. "Yes. I don't understand why you're getting so upset. You told me to tell you if I needed to stop."

"Not every five minutes."

"You don't need to yell at me."

Conley growled and restarted the bike. Without another word, he gunned the Harley. Jo jerked back. She grabbed hold of his waist and yelled into his ear. "I need to call my parents when we stop again."

She scooted so she wasn't plastered against his body and kept her hands lightly on his waist. Once her fear of the bike left her, she found the ride exhilarating and wished she could take off the helmet. She contemplated doing so and disregarded it as she stared at Conley's back. He wouldn't stop to let her.

Unwelcome thoughts of Blake rose in her mind. He'd beaten her severely enough to send her to the hospital when Jo's pregnancy expanded her waistline to an extent he thought disgusting. Jo had thought for sure she'd lose the baby.

Blake had told everyone she'd been in a car accident, even going so far as to run her car into a tree to back up his story. When she'd been released from the hospital, he'd reverted back to the loving husband he wished the world to see. Life behind the doors of their home had been different.

He'd spread the story that Alex was premature and had set strict guidelines in place of the baby's role in the home, acting the part of a doting father only when there were people around to witness the masquerade.

Jo had struggled to be the perfect trophy wife. She hadn't wanted to give Blake any reason to harm her baby. When his temper started to flare toward the little boy, she'd fled. Leaving no trace of her whereabouts until she'd sent that postcard.

She pounded her thigh. Stupid! She'd put Alex in danger because she'd felt guilty about running off without letting her parents know she was okay. She threw her hands in the air and grabbed Conley's waist again when she felt herself slide to the side.

As he weaved the bike in and out of traffic on the freeway, Jo's mind wandered, this time bringing Alex's face into focus. Tears welled again as she saw the curly brown hair and big, dark eyes. In her mind, he smiled, melting her heart, and she laid her head against Conley's back, allowing the tears to flow unchecked.

*

Conley shifted, shrugging his shoulders as Jo's

helmet bit between his shoulder blades. He straightened his back, trying to ease the uncomfortable pressure of her helmet. She turned her head, digging it in farther.

He exhaled sharply and resigned himself to two more hours of a fiberglass helmet digging into his spine. The stinging wind as they whipped down the interstate blurred his vision and he blinked rapidly.

He had to get another helmet once they reached Vegas. Who would have thought he'd be getting married? Jo was a sweet little thing, but she did try his patience sometimes. How did she manage to stay hidden for five years? Although it took a lot of courage to run off like she'd done, she didn't strike him as a very strong type of woman. He'd be finding out soon enough.

The sign welcoming them to Vegas loomed ahead.

6

"Mother? It's me."

"Jocelyn? Where are you? Your father and I have been so worried."

Jo leaned forward until her forehead laid flush against the plexi-glass panel of the phone booth. The grit accumulating there made her flesh crawl, and she stepped back, grimacing. The stench of urine and vomit flooded over her. Her stomach heaved, and she breathed through her mouth.

The door to the booth opened and Conley squeezed into the small space behind her. Her face heated. She tried moving into the corner away from him. There wasn't enough room. She sighed. "What, Mother? I didn't hear you."

Conley brushed against her. A tingling sensation rose in the pit of her stomach. Her body tensed. She wanted to kick herself for the range of emotions welling in her. She tossed him a look. "Get back."

Shaking his head, he gave her a slow, lazy smile. "I'm protecting you." He leaned his head closer to the handset.

"Jocelyn!"

"I'm sorry." She turned away and forced herself to focus on her mother's voice.

"Who's there with you?" Her mother's voice was loud, apprehensive.

"The man you hired to shadow me." She fought back her anger. Her knuckles whitened as she tightened her grip on the phone.

"Oh, good. He found you. Now come home."

"I *am* coming home. But only to get my son." Jo closed her eyes and leaned back against the wall of the old fashioned phone booth, ignoring the dirty graffiti and rust. "Blake stole him."

"It's not stealing when it's your own son." Her mother's sigh floated across the air waves.

"I told you Alex isn't Blake's son."

"Blake's marrying you was that boy's salvation, Jocelyn. He's the devil's own spawn. Blake should be rewarded for giving that boy his name."

"That *boy's* name is Alex, and he's your grandson." Related to you in more ways than one, Jo added mentally.

"Blake is a good husband, Jocelyn. A good provider. He's an upstanding..."

Jo sighed and opened her eyes. "I'm through talking to you. If you see Blake, tell him..."

"Let me speak to that man with you."

She handed the phone to Conley and tried to squeeze past him. With his free arm, he reached out and pulled her close. Although she found herself growing more conscious of his virile appeal, and the feelings caused her to grow increasingly uncomfortable, she felt very safe in the shelter of his arm. Almost as if she'd been created just for that reason. To be sheltered under Conley's wing. Her anxiety from speaking with her mother began to dissipate.

"Yes, ma'am," Conley drawled. "I'll be sure to...that is what you're paying me for." He smiled down at Jo and rolled his eyes. "With my life."

"What?" Jo met his gaze.

He smiled again. That lazy smile which made her heart flip-flop. "I'm to bring you home where you belong--and to protect you. Oh, yeah. Your father sends his love."

Jo slammed open the phone booth door. It banged into Conley's elbow.

"Ow!" He rubbed his elbow and cast an irritated glance her way.

"Sorry." She rushed over to the waiting Harley.

"I've got to get a helmet. I'm tired of bugs in my teeth."

Jo folded her arms across her chest. "She makes me so angry."

"Your mother?"

She nodded. "She doesn't listen. She can't see past his suave exterior. My mother thrills over the fact I lived in a two million dollar house and drove a BMW. I wore designer clothes and had a live-in nanny." She kicked at a can on the sidewalk. It clattered into the gutter.

Conley stepped closer to her and she shrugged him off. "Don't touch me. You're always touching me." She regretted the words the instant she saw his face fall. She reached out to him. "I'm sorry."

He held his hands up and stepped back. "I'm fine with it. I've always been a little too personal with people. Getting into their space." He handed her the helmet. "We need to go. It'll be dark soon, and we've got a lot to do."

"Conley, I..." she stopped as he held up his hand.

"Don't, Jo. I'm fine. Really." He mounted the bike. "Let's go."

"Conley, there's something you should know. Something that would explain why..."

"Later." He looked around them, motioning to the throngs of people milling around the sidewalk. "This isn't the place for personal revelations."

She nodded and placed the helmet on her head. Sighing, she slung her leg over the bike and scooted into place behind him.

*

Ouch. Conley's heart plummeted to his stomach. *I touched a raw nerve there. A bit surprised that it bothers me so much.* He revved the bike into gear and squinted against the sun's painful glare off the asphalt. He slowed and pulled alongside the sidewalk next to a motorcycle apparel store. "Stay here."

Jo nodded and kept her head down.

He returned ten minutes later and handed Jo a fluorescent pink helmet with an amber-colored face plate. "No hard feelings?"

The smile on her face when she removed the black helmet lit up his world.

"This is the gaudiest thing I've ever seen." Jo laughed.

"Yeah, but isn't it fun?"

"Glorious." She donned the new helmet and pulled down the face plate. "How do I look?"

"Like a true biker chick. Now for some indecently short shorts and a halter-top and you'd really look the part. Not to mention the coronary you'd give your parents."

She laughed again, low and throaty. His heart pounded against his ribs.

He donned the black helmet and popped the motorcycle in gear. He drove down the street toward an inexpensive hotel he'd stayed in on a previous trip to Las Vegas. He steered the bike beneath the overhang of the pink salmon colored Spanish style building. After securing the motorcycle, he loosely held Jo's elbow and steered her inside.

"One room," Conley told the desk clerk. "We're getting married."

The clerk looked up impassively and handed them a room key. "Everybody does. Do you want the room by the hour or for the night?"

Jo's eyes widened and she opened her mouth to speak. Conley put a finger to her lips. "For the night."

He took the key from the clerk and led Jo outside. The hotel was one story and laid out in an L shape. A white railing separated the rooms from the parking lot. The wind picked up, blasting them with heat and dust. They passed a cracked and drained swimming pool which sported mildew stains in its plaster.

Their room, number seven, lay at the end of the corridor. "A good number," Conley said.

Jo snorted and folded her arms across her chest. Once the door opened, she pushed past Conley and halted so quickly inside the room that he ran into her.

"Ow!" Jo grabbed her foot and hopped. "You stepped on my heel."

Reaching behind him, he closed the door. "Sorry. You shouldn't stop like that. Why did you?"

"The shock of the room, I guess."

He looked at the orange and purple paisley bedspread, the green shag carpet, and cheap reproduction art prints of desert scenes on the wall. "I don't remember it looking this bad."

"Came here a lot did you? By the hour?" Jo perched on the edge of the bed.

Conley tossed their bags on the bed and walked toward the bathroom. "Never brought anyone here." He knocked the door open. It banged against the wall with a thud. "I was never with the same person long enough to take them anywhere." He peeked around the corner. "Shower?"

Jo waved him off. "You can go first."

He waited what seemed eons before the water from the shower grew hot. He left his clothes in a huddle on the floor and stepped behind the vinyl curtain.

Butterflies fluttered in his stomach as the hot water washed over his face and down his shoulders. Although it was in name only, the thought of getting married scared him. His heart raced like an out of control thoroughbred. What if they couldn't get an annulment? Maybe he didn't understand the law. What if Jo, classy Jocelyn, were stuck with him?

He rested his forehead against the fiberglass wall and allowed the water to flow over his shoulders and cascade down the sore muscles of his back. Thoughts zipped through his brain, one after another, gathering speed as fast as a tornado. He banged his head softly against the shower wall.

Jo's face rose to the forefront of his mind. The dark auburn curls, shot through with threads of gold. The chocolate brown eyes with flecks as bright as the stars in the sky threatened to drown him in their sorrow. The mouth with a bottom lip fuller than the top. This line of thought would get him nowhere and accomplish nothing but fill him with frustration.

He turned off the water and stepped from the shower. He wrapped the largest of the threadbare bath towels around his waist. He stepped over the pile of his discarded clothing and opened the door.

*

Jo sat on the edge of the queen-size bed and stared at the carpet between her feet. An interesting stain spread across the cheap fibers. Its shape reminded her of the state of Texas. She giggled and took a deep breath, willing her racing heart to slow.

She sat and listened to the water run in the shower. *I should just get up and leave. Find my own way to Prestige. Rescue Alex and disappear again.* She sighed. *But I'm tired of fighting this on my own, and Conley seems so capable.*

Rising from the bed, she took two steps toward the hotel room door. She had no money-- no mode of transportation. She walked back to the bed and flopped belly first across it. She was stuck marrying a man she didn't know, following his lead, and taking his protection. It galled her.

She rolled over to her back and pounded the bed with both hands. She needed to keep moving. Get to Prestige--and to Alex. Tears escaped her eyes and rolled down her cheek. She swiped them away. No more crying.

The bathroom door opened, and she leaped from the bed. She gasped as Conley exited the bathroom clad only in a towel.

"For crying out loud, couldn't you get dressed first?" Didn't he have any idea what walking around like that would do to a woman? She peered into the bathroom. "And couldn't you have picked up your clothes? I'm not your maid."

He took a step back. "I'll pick them up, and my clean clothes are out here."

She stormed over to their satchel bag and yanked the zipper down. "See how difficult it is to get your clothes first? What are you an exhibitionist?" She reached in and pulled out a light blue dress. "I'll be out in a minute."

"O-kay." Conley drew out the word, clearly mystified at her behavior.

She slammed the door behind her, leaned against it, and then rested her head back. Again the tears threatened to flow, making her angrier at her weakness.

She kicked the pile of Conley's clothing on her way to the tub and spotted his razor on the edge of the tub. She smiled. After all, it's her wedding day. Couldn't have stubble, could she?

Turning on the faucet, she poured a liberal amount of the supplied shampoo under the running water. She let her clothes fall to the floor to join Conley's and stepped into the tub full of white shampoo bubbles. Taking up the razor and sliver of soap, she set to work shaving her legs.

The clean smell of the soap, and the rhythmic movements of her hand, lulled her into a sense of peace. The overwhelming feelings of anxiousness slid away with the rinsing of the suds.

The tub drain gurgled as the last of the water drained out. She toweled off briskly, tousling the curls on her head. She thought of tying them back then decided against it, leaving them instead to brush against her shoulders. She slipped the dress over her head, took a deep breath, and opened the door.

Conley was dressed in a clean pair of jeans and navy button up shirt when she exited the bathroom. He looked up to meet her gaze and gave a whistle of appreciation. "Wow."

She could second his reaction. The man looked good enough to eat. She smoothed the skirt of the flowing gauzy dress and twisted. It swirled around her knees. "I've always loved this dress. It makes me feel pretty." She locked gazes with him. "I'm sorry for my attitude. I'm nervous and scared, but that's no reason to take it out on you."

He patted her shoulder as he squeezed past her to the sink to squirt a handful of shaving cream into his hand and spread it across his face. He picked up his razor from the side of the tub and made a long swipe down his cheek. He drew in a sharp breath. A small bead of blood rose on his chin.

Jo laughed and clamped a hand across her mouth.

Conley frowned at her through the mirror. His eyes traveled to her bare legs. "Did you shave with my razor?"

She nodded and laughed. "I'm sorry. I know I shouldn't have. It was just a small way to get back at you for leaving your clothes on the floor."

"I told you I would pick them up." He held up

the razor. "What am I supposed to shave with?"

"Don't shave. You look cute with a shadow."

He threw the razor into the trash and wiped the cream from his face. "Great. Fine. A shadow with a clean line down one side." He scooped up the pile of dirty clothes and shoved them into a plastic bag someone had left in the room. He then stuffed them into their satchel. "There. Happy?"

Jo plopped on the bed. The bed springs squeaked. "I have to tell you something."

"Okay."

"My real name is Jocelyn Nielson."

"I know that. Why are telling me now?"

"I don't want the justice of the peace to call me by the wrong name."

"I wouldn't have let that happen." He shook his head. "What do you take me for?"

"I don't take you for anything. I don't even know you."

"Okay," Conley sucked in his cheeks. "My favorite color is, don't laugh, pink. Not a very manly color, but…there you go. I don't have a favorite food. I like it all. My parents were named Horace and Alice. Thank God, they didn't name me after my father."

He sat in the chair across from Jo. "They're dead now. A car accident two years ago. I'm an only child and somewhat of a disappointment to them. My middle name is Joseph. I'm thirty-one years old and my Christian faith is very important to me. Anything else you want to know?" He crossed his arms across his chest.

Jo shook her head, eyes wide. She lowered her gaze to the floor as heat spread across her face.

"Your favorite color is blue. Royal blue to be precise. You love Italian food, according to your mother, and your middle name is Edna. Named after an aunt. You're twenty-six years old. Your husband…"

"Ex-husband," she interrupted.

"Is quite a bit older than you. He's thirty-nine." He laughed when Jo wrinkled her nose. He lowered his voice. "And, although you believe in God, the most important thing to you is your son."

Tears welled in her eyes. "How do you know all this?"

"Lucky guess." He stood and held out his hand. "Do you want to get something to eat before we get married?"

7

Married. There was that word again. What was Jo thinking? "I could eat. Maybe." And she might just choke on the food.

"I know a great restaurant," Conley told her. "It's not far from here or from the chapel. We can walk so you won't get messed up on the bike."

"Okay."

"You all right?" His blue eyes were full of concern when he looked at her.

Jo nodded again. "As well as can be expected."

With his hand grasping her arm, Conley led her to the lobby of the hotel. Soft rock music issued from speakers mounted in the ceiling. Plastic ferns sat in cheap pots around the room. Stained Mexican tile spread under their feet.

A newspaper lying on a coffee table caught her attention. "Alex," she whispered.

She snatched the paper. On the front page was a picture of a smiling Blake, his arm around her son. The headline read "National Millionaire Overjoyed to Bring Missing Son Home. Wife Still Gone." A sob caught in her throat as Jo handed the paper to Conley.

"This is good news," he said after reading it.

"How?" She silently begged him to calm her, to reassure her.

"He's openly told people Alex is home. If anything happens to your son now, there will be questions." He set the paper back on the table. "I don't know what he plans to do, but I think Alex is safe."

"Thank God." Her legs gave way beneath her.

Conley helped her sit on the worn hotel sofa, then knelt in front of her. "Jo, this will—"

"I need a phone."

"Jo?"

"I need to use a phone. Right now, Conley."

"Okay." He rose and went to the desk clerk. He returned moments later with a cordless phone.

Jo grabbed it from his hands and punched in the numbers. "Blake. Let me talk to Blake."

"Jocelyn. It's good to hear your voice, Sweetheart. Are you ready to come home?"

"Don't patronize me. What do you think you're doing? Give me back my son. How dare you steal him?" Her voice rose.

"Come home where you belong, and you can have your son." Blake's voice was soft, matter-of-fact.

"He's *my* son, Blake. Not yours." Against her

will, Jo's voice trembled.

"And you're *my* wife."

"Not anymore," her voice quaked.

Blake sighed. "That was a mistake, Sweetheart. You're confused. Misled. You hurt me."

"Like you've hurt me?"

"Let me help you. Come home, and I will shower you with everything your little heart desires." His voice seeped like syrup and threatened to drown her in its stickiness.

"You're crazy. You just want to control me."

"Don't call me that!"

Click.

Jo stared at the receiver in her hand.

"He hung up on me."

Conley sat on the sofa next to her and placed his arm along the back of the sofa. "What did he say?"

"That it was a mistake to divorce. He wants me back." She leaned forward and placed her face in her hands. "He's using Alex to get me back."

"Why does he want you back?"

She stared at him, her body rigid. "Excuse me? Why wouldn't he want me back?"

Conley moved his arm around her shoulder and changed tactics. "What do you want to do?"

"I want to get married." She stood in front of him. "Let's go through you're your plan. Don't you see, Conley? If I'm married to you, he won't be able to force me to remarry him."

"He can't force you to do anything, Jo."

"I thought you wanted to marry me."

"I do."

"Then let's go eat." She marched out the door and waited on the sidewalk.

It was several minutes before Conley joined her. "Ready?" She turned.

He nodded and placed a hand on her lower back. Her nerves quivered under his touch. They walked the two blocks to the restaurant without speaking.

Conley opened the double glass doors and waved her in before him. A young girl wearing a white blouse and tie with black slacks greeted them with a smile.

"A table for two," Conley told the hostess. He smiled down at Jo as the young girl led them to a booth in the back of the restaurant and handed them their menus with a promise to return in a few minutes.

Classical music serenaded them. The strains rose above the muted sounds of the other patron's conversation. Occasionally, soft laughter rang forth, or a glass would clink. A utensil clattered against a porcelain plate. Tantalizing smells of beef and chicken wafted across the room.

Jo transferred her attention to the menu, pleased to discover they had a large variety of meal selections. When the waitress returned, Conley ordered steak, medium-rare, and she ordered a large chicken salad.

The cardboard coaster beneath her glass of water soon lay in tattered shreds as she dug at it with her fingernails. Once she'd finished with that, she fiddled with her eating utensils, rearranging them on the table. She glanced up to catch Conley watching her.

"What?"

"Nothing." Conley lifted his glass of soda to his mouth.

"What?"

He set the glass heavily on the table. Water sloshed over the rim. "What are you doing, Jo? If you're this nervous, call it off. Maybe it's a dumb idea. I just thought...since Blake has the town in the palm of his hand...well, we don't need to do this."

Jo frowned. "I'm not nervous."

"Yes you are. You're biting the inside of your cheek. You do that when you're nervous. And you're shredding every piece of paper in sight."

She stuck her nose in the air. "How do you know what I do when I'm nervous?"

"I've been studying everything about you for weeks." He took another gulp of his soda. "You'd be surprised at what I know."

"That's creepy. Stop it." She sat back in the booth and allowed the waitress to place her plate on the table.

"No," he said. "It's fun." He picked up his fork and knife and sliced into the steak. When the meat was cut into bite size pieces, he twisted the plate a fraction of a turn and dug his fork into his mashed potatoes.

Jo held her fork suspended in mid-air as she watched him eat. "Why do you do that?"

"Do what?" he asked around a mouthful of food.

"You cut your steak then turned your plate to eat your potatoes. Then you turned your plate again to eat your vegetables."

"I didn't want my potatoes to get cold." He speared a piece of steak. "And I like saving the best for last."

Jo raised her eyebrows and shrugged. She looked around the restaurant and paid more attention to the white linen tablecloths and well-dressed patrons. "This is an expensive place? Can you afford it?"

"It's our wedding dinner. Don't worry about it."

"Exactly how much does a private investigator make?"

"Stop being a snob." His fork clattered against his plate.

"I am not, nor have I ever been, a snob." Her voice rose. A couple sitting at a table close to them glanced their way. She lowered her voice. "How dare you say that!"

"How dare *you* assume I can't afford a place like this." Conley plopped back against the cushioned backrest and folded his arms across his chest. His eyes focused for a moment on a spot somewhere behind her. Finally meeting her gaze, he answered. "$75.00 an hour, plus expenses. I'm making a bundle off your parents. In fact, they're paying for this meal."

"Good." Jo dug into her salad with a relish.

Conley remained silent for a minute then

laughed. Softly at first then escalating into a loud guffaw. He snorted. "Sorry."

Jo set her fork on the side of the plate and frowned. "What's so funny?"

"You." He wiped his eyes with his napkin. "I haven't laughed like this in years. You're good for me." He snorted again and excused himself from the table.

She looked around the restaurant as Conley walked, laughing, to the men's room. People stared at her, frowns on their faces. Blushing, she shrugged and ducked her head.

*

Conley still laughed as he pushed open the door to the restroom. He strolled to the wide mirror and stared at his red face. Shaking his head, he turned on the cold water and splashed his face.

Someone grabbed a handful of his hair and slammed his head into the mirror. Spots danced before him, obscuring his vision. Before he could act, a knee slammed into his stomach. He dropped to the floor.

When his attacker lifted his leg to kick, Conley grabbed the man's foot and twisted. The man hit the floor with a thud. Taking a gulp of air into tortured lungs, Conley threw himself on top of his attacker. He smashed his forearm into the man's windpipe.

"Who are you?" He stared down into dark eyes. The man's ebony hair, long and greasy, splayed across the tiled floor.

The man arched his back, knocking Conley off. He scrambled to his feet and whipped a switchblade from his tattered jeans.

Conley crab-walked backward until he could regain his footing. He held his hands loosely in front him.

"There's no need for that." He kicked the weapon from the man's hand. It landed with a resounding clatter on the tile.

His attacker rushed forward and head-butted him in the face. Blood ran down Conley's chin and dripped onto his shirt.

"Now you've done it. I'm getting married in this shirt." He thrust his fist forward, busting the other man's nose. The bone crunched beneath his fist and blood spurted. Conley grabbed him in a headlock before dragging the man through the receiving door of the restaurant. He tossed him down the small flight of cement stairs.

"I don't know who you are or why you've chosen me as your victim." Conley's voice was low and even. "But I'm not a man you want to mess with." He wiped an arm across his lips and watched the other man stumble to his feet. The stranger turned and scampered down the alley.

Conley headed back to the men's room. He removed his shirt and scrubbed at the blood spots with a paper towel. When he'd cleaned as much of it from his shirt as he could, he again splashed his face with cold water, then held the wet shirt under the hand dryer.   An older man in a well-tailored suit entered the restroom and paused, looking at the shirtless man.

Conley grinned. "Spilled my gravy."

The man nodded without speaking and disappeared into one of the stalls.

Conley donned his damp, wrinkled shirt, and headed back to the table.

Jo's eyes widened when she spotted him. "That was some bathroom break. Why's your shirt wet?"

"Had to wash the gravy out." Conley tossed money beside his empty plate.

"You don't have gravy. What happened to your lip?"

"I ran into the door laughing." He grabbed her arm and pulled her from her chair. The chair fell to the floor, the sound loud in the quiet room. "Time to go."

She sputtered as he dragged her from the crowded restaurant. Once outside she jerked her arm free. "What is going on?"

"Nothing." He looked down at her standing with her hands on her hips. "We want to get to the chapel before it closes."

"I don't think the chapels close here in Vegas, at least not for a while yet." She planted her feet. "I'm not moving until you tell me what happened to your lip."

He pulled her into an alcove. "At least get out of the middle of the sidewalk."

"Well?"

"Somebody hit me."

"Somebody hit you." Her eyes widened. "In the restroom."

"That's what I said."

"Why?"

"How should I know? He just came up behind me and hit me. Slammed my head into the mirror. I think I have a bump." He reached up to feel his forehead.

"You have a cut on your chin and if you don't stop beating around the bush," Jo said. "I'm going to give you a bump. A big one."

He flexed his shoulders and rotated his head, trying to loosen the kinks. "I was washing my face when someone came up behind me and attacked me. I've never seen him before."

"Well, did you ask him who he was?"

"Of course I did!" His brows furrowed as he stared at her. "What do you take me for—a fool?"

She bent forward, just a bit. "I take you for a private investigator. A good one, according to you. If you're so good, how could someone sneak up behind you in a public restroom and beat you senseless?" She turned away from him and folded her arms across her chest.

He opened his mouth, only to snap it closed again. He found himself at a loss for words. A rarity.

She whirled to face him. "Well? Are we going?"

He nodded and took her arm more gently this time, and led her to a small, white, quaint chapel. White pillars flanked the double white doors. White pots on the small porch held white silk flowers. A small non-obtrusive sign with gold lettering stated simply 'Chapel'.

"Thank you," Jo said.

"For what?"

"I thought you were going to take me someplace like the Elvis chapel." She smiled up at Conley. "This is cute. Not tacky at all."

"Thought you'd like it." He pushed open the doors and steered her inside where a smiling, large busted blonde beamed at them from behind a desk.

"Welcome. Getting married?" she cooed.

Jo fluttered her lashes and looked away. Conley gave her a little pinch on the tender underside of her arm. "Be nice." He returned the blonde's smile. "Right away, please."

"You're in luck. The chapel is empty. Wait one moment and I'll return with the justice of the peace." She waved toward a display of flowers. "We have fresh or silk bouquets for sale. Feel free to browse." The woman's exaggerated wiggle as she walked away made him smile. Jo scowled at him.

He chose a bouquet of pink roses, baby's breath, and ferns. He handed them to Jo with a wink and a smile.

She buried her face in the blossoms and took a deep breath. "Thank you."

"You're welcome." *You're beautiful.*

"We're ready for you," Blondie said. She poked her head through the swinging doors.

Jo started to enter the doors, and Conley held her back. "Wait. Would you walk down the aisle to me?" His voice barely rose above a whisper. "I know it's a marriage of convenience, but, well, I've never been married before and..."

Her brown eyes met his. "If you'd like."

Feeling shy all of a sudden, he answered. "I'd like it very much." He flashed a quick grin and ducked through the doors.

Frigid air hit him as he stepped into the chapel, and he shivered. He marched to the smiling man dressed in a dark suit who waited for him at the front. Conley stood beside him and turned.

His breathing quickened as the wedding march sounded and the doors opened electronically. Jo hesitated for only a moment, her hand at her throat. Her tell-tale sign of tightening bronchial tubes. She took a deep breath before taking a step toward him.

Conley pulled the inhaler he'd snatched from the night stand from his pocket and held it in his palm. Jo's eyes widened before she giggled. Her cheeks reddened. The tension lines eased on her face.

He admired the gold glints in her hair as she strode toward him. The twig of baby's breath she'd stuck there made him smile.

Her hands shook as she handed the bouquet to the one he'd dubbed Blondie. She shook her head at the offered inhaler. Conley dropped it back into his pocket before he reached to take her hand. His gaze remained glued to her face as the justice of the peace spoke the wedding vows over them.

Voice shaking, Conley repeated his vows and removed the small gold ring he wore on his pinky. His fingers trembled as he placed the ring on Jo's finger and bent to kiss her. His eyes closed. He brushed his lips across hers. Her small intake of breath caused his heart to skip a beat. He was a lost man, drowning in the wake of a beautiful, hurting woman.

8

The sight of the double bed in the hotel room stopped Jo in mid-stride. Her throat constricted, and she fought to swallow past the lump. When they'd left, they'd kept the bathroom light on and now it shone with an intimate glow across the shag carpet

Conley stood so close behind her she felt his body heat. "Don't worry," he whispered. His breath stirred the hair behind her ear and sent shivers down her spine. "I'll sleep on the floor."

She turned and bumped her nose on his chest. Without looking up, she said, "I have to tell you something. I need to tell you who Alex's father is."

"Okay."

She led the way farther into the room and sat cross-legged on the bed, tucking the bottom of her dress beneath her.

"May I?" Conley gestured to the spot next to

her.

She nodded as he lay on his side and propped his head on his hand.

"You don't have to tell me anything."

"I know, but you deserve to know why I'm so prickly. Why I pull away from you so much. Why I jump when you touch me."

"I thought it was my animal magnetism."

She tilted her head and glared. How could he joke when she was trying to be serious?

"Sorry. I'm a stranger. I get it."

"It's more than that." She shook her head and stared into his eyes. He smiled. One corner of his mouth hitched, inviting her to confide in him.

"There's a lot I don't remember from the years before I married Blake. Parts of it are dark. Things I've blocked out, I guess." She took a shaky breath. "My mother's brother, my uncle, is named Dave." Jo ran a hand through her hair. "This is difficult."

Conley reached over and engulfed her hand with his. "You don't have to tell me."

"My uncle had been 'visiting' me for as long as I can remember," she blurted. If she thought about it, paused, she'd never get the words out. "Every time he visited, I'd freeze up. Do whatever he told me to." Her words faded to a whisper. "He said he'd kill me if I told anyone. Alex is his son."

"Do your parents know?"

She shook her head. "I never told them. I didn't think they would believe me." She rose from the bed.

She walked to the window and parted the curtains to peer out. What if Black had sent someone to follow them back to Prestige? "You see how they are with my ex-husband. They'll believe anyone over me. My mother just believes I was a wanton teenager, forsaking everything she'd taught me."

Tears rolled down her cheeks. "I feel like a weak idiot. Letting it continue even after I became an adult." She slapped the window and banged her forehead against the glass. "He frightens me. Even now, after I've been gone all these years, Dave and Blake haunt my dreams." She turned back to face him. "I don't mean to be cruel to you, Conley. I find it hard to trust people. I went from my uncle to Blake. Blake was my husband, but he acted as if he owned me. Do you know how that can be? I wasn't his wife, I was his possession."

Conley rose from the bed and wrapped his arms around her. He pulled her close and held her head to his chest. For several minutes she cried silently, listening to the beat of his heart.

"I won't let anyone hurt you again," he said, his words soft.

"I wish I could believe that." She wanted to, but no man had ever proven trustworthy in her life. Conley seemed different, and she realized how useful he could be as her husband when she confronted Blake, but total trust…she wasn't sure she was capable.

"Jo." He tilted her face up to his. As he lowered his mouth to kiss her, the phone rang. Its shrill brrring separated them as effectively as if someone had stepped between them.

Jo walked to the phone, her steps heavy, and lifted the receiver on the fourth ring.

"Did I interrupt something, Jocelyn?"

"Blake."

"Who is the man in your room?" His cold voice sliced through the phone.

"Where are you?" She parted the curtains and peered out into the gathering darkness. "Can you see me?"

"No, but my man can. It's amazing what money will buy. I'll repeat, Jocelyn, who is the man in the room with you?"

"My husband," she whispered. "He's my husband." She slid to the floor and reached to clutch at Conley's hand. He grasped hers and knelt beside her.

"Your husband. Well, well, well. You do work fast. The man in my employ said he'd seen you enter a chapel. I refused to believe it. Your parents will be so disappointed."

Jo listened to his breathing. Her heart laid heavy in her chest. She squeezed Conley's hand.

"Well, I knew the type of woman I married." Blake's voice lacked emotion. "The fact you were pregnant when we wed branded you the trollop you seem to be." He sighed heavily. "I had such hopes for you, my dear."

"Let me talk to Alex."

"I don't think so."

"Please." Her words shook. "He's my son."

"Say goodbye, Jocelyn."

"Mommy." Her son's voice shrieked in her ear. "Mommy, where are you?"

"Alex." Jo bolted to her feet, not letting go of Conley's hand.

Blake got back on the phone. "I have the upper hand here, my dear. I suggest you annul your marriage and get back home where you belong."

Click.

"I can't believe he keeps hanging up on me." Jo stared at the silent receiver in her hand.

Conley took the receiver from her hand and placed it back in its cradle. He lowered her to the edge of the bed and stared into her eyes. "Talk to me."

"He threatened me with Alex." She looked at him. "Told me to say goodbye." She glanced toward the window. "He has someone watching us. He knows where we are."

"It'll be all right." Conley rose and went to the window.

A shot ripped through the night, showering them with glass from the shattered window. A woman screamed, high and shrill. At first Jo didn't realize it was her, but then Conley spun and fell to the floor.

Blood welled from a wound in his shoulder. Crimson soaked the blue fabric of his shirt. She dropped to her knees beside him and pulled his head into her lap. What had she done? By marrying him, she'd signed his death certificate. "Conley."

"I'm here." He struggled to a sitting position.

"The bullet just grazed me. I was already turning when he shot."

"Let me see." Jo pulled at his shirt, popping buttons and Conley laughed. "What's so funny?"

"I've always dreamed of a woman ripping my shirt off. Just never thought it would be under these circumstances."

"Very funny." She eased the shirt from his wounded arm. A deep furrow ran across the flesh of his upper arm. "That's more than a graze. It'll need stitches. We'll have to go to the hospital."

"Can't."

Sirens wailed in the distance.

"We've got to go now. Grab your stuff." He rolled to his knees, holding his arm against his side.

Jo frowned. "At least let me wrap it for you. You're bleeding."

He yanked the pillow case from the pillow and handed it to her. "Tie it around my arm. As tight as you can."

When she'd finished, he pushed to his feet. He rushed to the saddlebag and grabbed a clean tee shirt. He pulled it over his head and grimaced as he pushed his arm through the sleeve. "Hurry."

"What if the shooter is still out there? Let the police catch him."

"We'll take our chances. If the police get here, we'll be detained. It'll take us longer to get to Alex. There will be a lot of questions. Do you want that?"

"No, but..."

He tossed her the saddlebag and opened the door. With a stern look, he jerked his head toward outside. Without another word Jo rushed outside, leaving Conley to grab their helmets. By the time he joined her, she was seated, saddlebag firmly in place. She slapped the helmet on her head, wrapped her arms tightly around Conley's waist, and they roared off.

Fully expecting a shot in the back, she tensed her shoulders, holding them rigid. The skirt of her dress flew, rising above her waist, blinding her. A horn blared and male voices jeered, only to be blown away on the wind rushing past. Conley glanced over his shoulder and the bike tottered. His shoulders shook as he laughed.

Struggling to keep her hold on his waist as they sped through the Vegas streets, Jo released one hand and gathered her dress in front of her. Her temper flared, and she gritted her teeth. She lost her grip on the dress as they careened around a corner. Once again, the dress billowed around her, sending the cool evening air up her back.

She sighed, her shoulders relaxing when Conley slowed the bike and drove into an alley. When Jo removed her helmet, she realized he was still laughing and slung the helmet at his back.

"Hey! I'm injured." He removed his own helmet and remained seated and grinned. "As much as I enjoyed the view, and I'm sure others did, I think you'd be more comfortable in pants."

"And *you're* still bleeding."

He looked down at the spreading stain through

the pillow case. "We'll stop at a drugstore, you can go in, grab supplies, and when we stop again I'll sit patiently while you nurse me, okay?"

"Nurse yourself." Jo pulled a pair of pants from the saddlebags. As she bent over to step into them a gust of wind blew the dress over her head. Exasperated, she straightened and glared at Conley, daring him to laugh.

It didn't work. By this time, Conley laughed so hard, he snorted.

Jo straightened, eyes narrowed. She pulled the pants up and zipped them. "If you're finished laughing at my demise, we can continue on our way."

"Sure." He snorted again, replacing his helmet. "Shame to hide that view, though."

She glanced at the stain on his shirt and lifted her chin.

"You wouldn't."

"Wouldn't I?"

"You're not that mean."

"Aren't I?" She swung her helmet at him.

Conley deflected it with his uninjured arm. "You win," he said, lowering his face plate. "You have me at a distinct disadvantage."

"And don't forget it." She swung her leg over the bike and took her seat behind him.

*

Conley maneuvered them back into the Vegas traffic and headed toward the freeway. His mind retrieved the image of her barely covered bottom, pale in the gloom of the alley, and he chuckled, catching himself before Jo could pound on his back. That sight was worth taking a bullet for. He grinned.

They stopped at a small drugstore where Jo ran in and returned moments later with a plastic bag. Soon, they pulled into a smaller, more ramshackle motel than they'd been in previously. Conley sent Jo inside the manager's office.

"I got a room with two beds," she said, sliding on behind him. "It's on the other side of the hotel."

He nodded. His limbs trembled with fatigue. When he pulled into the empty space before their room, Jo slid off the bike first and scooted under his uninjured arm. "Let me help you."

She propped him against the wall of the building while she inserted the key into the lock and swung the door open. Once again taking his weight upon her shoulders, she helped him into the room and onto the closest bed, stepping back. "This is the ugliest room I've ever seen. I thought the last one was bad."

Two beds with flat gold bedspreads took up most of the space in the small room. One end table sat between the two beds with a wall-mounted lamp hanging over it. Faded, green flowered wallpaper covered the walls, one corner pulling free. A musky smell wafted up from the bedclothes. Conley wrinkled his nose.

"Sit up for a minute." She removed his helmet and tossed it onto the other bed. "Do you need help getting your shirt off?"

He shook his head and, arms shaking, pulled the shirt off. He lay back against the pillows as Jo lay out the supplies on the nightstand. The rough fabric of the gold bedspread itched his bare back.

She disappeared into the bathroom and returned with a folded towel which she placed under his injured arm. She uncapped the bottle of hydrogen peroxide and poured it liberally over his arm. He hissed.

"I almost bought iodine, just to be mean." Jo winked. "But my compassionate side reared up and wouldn't let me."

"Thank God you have a compassionate side. I was beginning to wonder."

She dabbed around the wound with a smaller towel. After opening a box of butterfly enclosures, she bent low over his arm. Her hair brushed his chest. Conley drew in a deep breath and inhaled a scent of warm golden tresses and Vegas evening air. She pinched the edges of the wound together and secured them with a few strips of the butterfly tape.

"Am I hurting you?" She raised her head. Concerned eyes peered into his.

"A little." Conley cupped the back of her head, gently entangling his hand in her hair, and pulled her closer. "But I know what would make me feel better."

"What?"

"This." He pulled her to meet his lips and lost himself for a moment in her softness. Her lips trembled beneath his, and his heart skipped a beat as she pulled slowly away.

"Better?" She took her bottom lip between her teeth, doing things to his insides better left in the recesses of his mind.

"Oh, yeah." He forced his breathing to remain regulated.

She got up and pulled a blanket from her bed and covered him. Bending over him, she placed a kiss on his forehead. "You should sleep. You feel warm. Let me get you some aspirin."

"I'm fine."

"I want to." She disappeared again, this time outside.

Conley raised himself to one elbow and waited anxiously for her to reappear. When she did, she carried an ice bucket and two plastic cups, and filled them at the sink. She got two aspirin from the bottle beside the bed and handed them to him, along with one of the cups.

"I'm sorry," she said, her voice barely above a whisper.

"What?"

"I'm sorry."

"I can't hear you. The bullet must have done something to my hearing."

"Conley."

He laughed. "It's okay. It was funny, and I won't deny I enjoyed it, but I shouldn't have laughed."

"Are we even talking about the same thing?" She perched on the bed next to him. "I would have done the same, if it would have been someone else flashing their nether regions." She looked toward the window. "But, I'm talking about putting you in danger. Do you think that man followed us?"

"I'm sure he did. If not, he knows which way we're headed. Don't leave the room again without me. Jo, I'm here of my own accord. Don't apologize."

"Alex sounded so scared. I wanted to gather him in my arms and hold tight."

Conley reached up and cupped her face with his hand. "We'll find him. He'll be all right. Blake put in the newspapers that Alex is home. He can't let him disappear now without a lot of questions."

Nodding, she stood and put the medical supplies back into the bag. Then she stuffed them in the saddlebags.

She moved to the other bed, pulled down the covers then slid fully clothed beneath them. She reached above her head for the chain on the lamp and tugged, plunging the room into the semi-darkness common to cheap hotel rooms.

She lay facing him, her eyes shadowed. He wasn't sure, but Conley thought he saw the glimmer of tears make their way down her cheeks. He ached to rise from his bed and go to her, pulling her close, giving her shelter, but the thought of moving that far made his wound ache.

Light glinted off the ring she wore on her left hand and joy rose in him. He was married. Maybe not in the way he thought he'd be, but God willing, Jo would grow to love him.

He rolled to his back, folding his uninjured arm and placing it behind his head. Staring at the ceiling, he allowed his thoughts to wrap around the fact they might have rescued Alex and annulled their marriage before her love could grow. The air left him in a rush. His fear of losing her crashed down upon him.

"Are you in pain?" Jo's voice drifted softly across the room.

Yes. "No, I'm fine." He turned his head to smile at her. "Just sighing. How are *you* doing?" *How are you doing?* Conley felt like punching himself in the head.

She giggled. The sound rippled through the room and lifted Conley's heart on its waves. "I'm fine. How's the weather over there?"

"Dry."

Her laughter held a touch of hysteria, and she wiped her eyes on the corner of her blanket. Within seconds, she sobbed, burying her face in the pillow.

Conley tossed his blanket aside. "Come here."

She shook her head. "It wouldn't be right."

"We're married. I'm just going to hold you. I'm in no physical condition for anything else." He patted the bed.

Hesitating for only a second, she slid from her bed and into his. He held his arm wide, inviting her to scoot close. When she did, snuggling up beneath his armpit and laying her head on his chest, Conley closed his eyes and worried what the next day would bring.

9

Blake slammed the phone into its cradle and glowered at the boy. Alex scurried to the corner of the room. "Relax, boy. I'm not going to hurt you."

He strode to the leather chair behind the massive oak desk and sat. The leather creaked beneath him. He twirled the ball point pen lying on the highly polished surface, then picked it up and brought it to his mouth. He tapped the end of the pen against his teeth.

Married. She couldn't marry. She belonged to him. He tossed the pen across the room, bouncing it off the 13 by 20 inch portrait of Jo hanging on the wall. Bolting to his feet, he paced, coming just inches from Alex.

The boy drew his legs closer to his body, and Blake smiled. "Don't be afraid of me. Without you, your mother would have no reason to return." He bent over to bring his face close to the boy's. "You have a new daddy now. Did I tell you?"

Alex wrapped his arms around his legs and rested his chin on top of his knees. "I hope he's nicer than you."

Blake's face moved closer, so close, he could feel the boy's breath on his face. "He won't be," he whispered. "He's tattooed and drives a motorcycle." He rose and stood before Jo's portrait. "She married a man so far beneath her, she'll need a scraper to get him off her shoe.

"But, then, she's not who I thought she was. She hasn't risen to my expectations." He doubled his fist with the intentions of striking the portrait. Thinking better of it, he spun on his heel and left the boy alone.

The first person his eyes fell upon in the hall was the boy's new tutor. A quiet, mousy woman. "Alex is in my office. Please remove him then send Rosarita to me."

"Yes, sir." The woman scurried past him. "Right away."

Blake stood, hands clasped behind his back, and waited for the woman to reemerge with the boy. A thin smile split his face when the boy stopped before him.

"I know who you're talking about," Alex said. "He went to the zoo and bought me and Mommy ice cream. He *is* nice." The boy stuck out his tongue and followed his tutor down the hall and away from Blake.

White hot anger engulfed Blake. He grabbed a Tiffany lamp from a side table and hurled it to the floor. With a curse, he slammed his fist into the wall. Shaking the pain free, he strode back to his office and picked up the phone.

*

The bugs were back. Once again Jo found herself in the dark.

Bugs crawled through her hair, into her mouth, and dropped from the ceiling above her. This time she found herself bound hand and foot and struggled to get free. She clamped her lips tightly together in order to prevent more of the nasty things from finding their way in. Whimpers escaped her throat.

A door opened and light burst through, blinding her. A heavy-set man stood shadowed there. "Are you ready to cooperate?" He advanced. His laugh bounced off the rock walls which surrounded her. He reached out...

"Jo."

She screamed and fought the hands that grabbed her shoulders. Her flailing hand connected with something, a face, and she raked her fingernails.

"Ow! It's me, Conley. It's only a dream. A nightmare. Wake up, sweetheart."

She opened her eyes. Conley's worried face leaned over her. Red tracks from her nails left shallow furrows down his cheek. She struggled to move only to find her legs entangled in the sheets, and she kicked harder to free herself. "Let go of me."

Conley raised his hands and sat back, his brow wrinkled. "Okay." He lifted a hand to his cheek.

After crawling from the bed, Jo sprinted to the

restroom and slammed the door behind her. She leaned her hands on the sink and stared at her reflection in the mirror. Perspiration dotted her forehead and upper lip. Her shirt clung to her shoulders and a trickle of sweat ran down her chest between her breasts.

Reaching over, she turned on the cold water faucet, letting it run full blast. Slipping her hands beneath the flow, she cupped them and lifted to bring the water to her face. Her hands shook, spilling some of the water down the front of her. Grunting, she whipped the shirt over her head and tossed it to the floor.

Her trembling increased as her stomach heaved, and she lurched toward the toilet, losing everything she'd eaten the night before. With a groan she slid to the floor. She drew up her knees and wrapped her arms around them.

The tile splashed wall behind her was cold on her back and the hooks of her bra dug into her skin. She contemplated moving, then thought otherwise as an attack of weakness came over her and she fell over on to her side, her clothes pillowed under her head. Tightness constricted her lungs.

"Jo?" Conley pushed the door open and peered inside. He scooped her into his arms. Murmuring endearments, he carried her to the bed.

He lay her down and went back to the bathroom, reappearing with a damp rag. Perched on the side of the bed, he wiped her face, smoothing her hair back. "What's wrong? Where is your inhaler?"

She shook her head and shrugged. "I don't

know. I have this dream sometimes where I'm in this room, it might be a cave, and I'm surrounded by insects. They're in my hair, my mouth, and under my feet." She shuddered. "I've never thrown up after having the dream before."

"Some dream." He smiled down at her. "How often do you have it?"

"More frequently lately. Used to be I'd only have it a couple of times a month." Blood seeped from beneath the butterfly enclosures on Conley's arm, Jo bolted up. "You're bleeding. You shouldn't have carried me. You've pulled it open."

"It's all right." He glanced down at his arm and flexed. "It's not bleeding much."

"Let me fix it." She swung her legs over the side of the bed and rose, desperate to escape his eyes which seemed to her to search her face, looking for something she couldn't give. Suddenly conscious of her state of dress, or lack thereof, her eyes widened. "Um…I need my clothes."

His eyes flicked toward the saddlebag, and he laughed. "I like what you're wearing."

Jo quickly unzipped the bag and grabbed a tee shirt and her inhaler. The shirt was wrinkled and stained. She pulled it over her head and took two puffs of her inhaler before digging out the medical supplies. She located the enclosures and sat back next to Conley. "Hold still."

She applied new enclosures to his wound, pulling the skin tight together before applying the tape.

"No more physical exertion. Not for a while."

"I'll agree to that if you'll agree to no more fainting."

"I didn't faint."

"You did. Right after you threw up." He reached up and tucked a curl behind her ear. "How do you feel now?"

"Fine. Hungry. Embarrassed." She stood. "Pick one."

He grabbed his shirt from the foot of the bed where he'd tossed it the night before. Raising it to his nose, he sniffed. "We need a change of clothes." He grinned up at her. "Wanna charge an outfit to your parents?"

Jo smiled back. "I'd love to. Several of them."

*

Conley took her to a small boutique on the outskirts of Vegas.

"This is a woman's clothing store. What about you?"

"There's a discount store right down the street. I just need a pair of jeans and a clean shirt."

"I won't have you meeting my parents in jeans. They'll eat you alive." Jo stood on the sidewalk and glanced up the street and down. "Oh, good. There's a men's clothing store. When I'm finished, we'll go shopping for you."

"Great." He flung a leg over the bike and removed his helmet. "I can't wait."

She stood looking up at him. "You need a

haircut, too."

"No, I don't. That's where I draw the line."

"But it touches your shoulders. It's almost as long as mine." She reached up and ran her fingers through his curls.

He shrugged and firmed his jaw. "No."

"Fine." She whirled and marched into the store. A disgruntled Conley followed.

He sat on a sofa too small for his large frame while she dug through racks of clothing. Item after item was handed to the sales clerk. "Where do you think we're going to put all that?"

"I'm not buying it all. But, I'm not showing up at my parents looking like a vagabond, either." She tossed one more blouse on the pile. "Be right out."

He raised his eyebrows and looked around. The boutique was small. The walls were that pinkish color women called mauve, heavy curtains hung from the windows, and love songs played in the background. Displays of cologne and jewelry stood next to the checkout. Conley groaned and tried to get comfortable on the flowered sofa. He stretched his long legs out before him.

"How's this?"

Jo stood before him dressed in a simple linen sheath dress of pale blue.

"Beautiful. Can we go now?"

"Wait. I need more things than just this dress. I don't want my parents to think I'm destitute."

"But you are destitute."

She frowned at him. "Don't be mean. It doesn't become you, besides it's been ages since I've been shopping like this."

"What do you think they'll say when they get the bill?" He scratched at the healing split on his chin. "Or when they see me? I'm cut up and shot."

"I don't care. You're going to look great. I'm not going to show up wrinkled and smelly with no clothes to my name. And neither are you."

"I've got clothes at home."

"Which is?"

"About forty minutes from here."

"Jeans and tee shirts."

He sighed heavily and rose to pace while she tried on another outfit. When she'd finished, she was richer by one blue sheath dress, some black filmy thing she didn't try on for him, white cotton slacks, assorted blouses and undergarments, one pair of jeans, and several shoes. She wore the jeans, a vintage tee shirt and ankle boots with ridiculously high heels.

"Ready?" She smiled.

Nodding, Conley waited while the salesclerk carefully folded each item in tissue paper and laid them in a box. He must be crazy. No doubt.

"You can tie the box on the bike, Conley. No problem." She handed him the box and pranced out of the store ahead of him. "Now it's your turn."

"Oh, goody."

He stood like a dope while Jo rattled off instructions to the clerk at the men's store. The clerk took his measurements, exclaiming over the size of his shoulders, tsk-tsking over his tattoos and wound, and then the man disappeared into a back room. Before Conley knew what hit him, he was laying out his charge card for a suit, pants, several polo shirts, designer jeans, and new alligator skin boots.

Jo wrote something down on a slip of paper and handed it to the clerk. "Two days?"

The man nodded.

Turning to Conley, she asked, "Can we be at my parents within two days?"

"Late tomorrow, if you want."

"Wonderful." She beamed at him. "You're going to knock them dead."

"They've already seen me, Jo." He followed her, carrying the now heavier box, back to his bike.

"Yes, they have. But not all cleaned up."

Conley tied the box with twine he'd borrowed from the men's store onto the bike, hoping, and hoping not, that it would fall and be lost somewhere on the highway. "You are definitely a snob."

"Caring what people think is not being a snob."

"Do you know how much money you spent today? Do you care?" He stared down at her. "One thousand dollars give or take a few hundred."

"So? You're not paying for it."

He shook his head, picking up his helmet. "A snob."

Jo climbed onto the back of the bike. "I need confidence when I confront Blake and my parents.

Those filthy wrinkled things I was wearing wasn't going to give it to me. Don't you ever feel like that?"

"God gives me my confidence." He latched his helmet and situated himself in front of her.

"Not the God I grew up with."

Conley jerked her hands tighter around his waist, popped the bike into ignition then eased them back onto the road. A disturbing thought tickled at the back of Conley's mind. Who exactly were her parents and what kind of childhood had Jo had?

10

Prestige hadn't changed much in the time Jo had been gone. Dusk fell and the turn of the century style street lights cast a welcoming glow, leading the town's citizens into a false sense of peace and security. If they only knew the evil that lurked behind some of the most expensive mansions.

The Harley growled down the one road that grandly called itself Main Street. Brick front buildings, lights muted for the night, lined both sides of the street. Trimmed evergreen bushes stood next to the sidewalks beside a park complete with a gazebo and ornamental fish pond.

A twitch developed behind Jo's left eye the further they drove into town. A dull throb began in the center of her forehead and spread behind her eyes and around to the back of her head. Her chest tightened. The thought of her inhaler safely in Conley's pocket reassured her and prevented an attack.

"There's a small hotel on the other side of town," she yelled. The action sent shards of pain through her skull. Conley nodded and turned in the direction she pointed.

Prestige, being a small town, only took minutes to drive through. Jo sighed as Conley stopped the bike, and she removed her helmet. She rubbed at the spot between her eyes.

"I'll get the room." Conley laid a hand on her shoulder. "Be right back."

She waited with hunched shoulders and bowed head. The throbbing increased, now shooting daggers through her eyes. She squinted against the street lamp's stab of light.

"Jocelyn Nielson?"

Raising pained eyes, Jo groaned. Standing beside her was a woman she'd graduated high school with. Meredith Burney stood in tight designer jeans, silky camisole, and stiletto heeled boots. Her dyed blonde hair was swept up and away from her face. Fuzzy strands trailed down her back.

"What are you doing here?" Meredith squealed. "Your husband has been looking everywhere for you. He's been worried sick." She cocked a hip, frowning.

"My *husband* is getting us a room."

Meredith's head whipped around. "Blake's here? Why?" She smiled. "Oh, a little private rendezvous to celebrate your homecoming?"

Jo sighed. "Meredith, since you seem so interested

in my life, I'm surprised you don't know Blake is no longer my husband. I've come back to Prestige to get my son." She glanced behind her former classmate. "What are you doing here? A little rendezvous of your own? I don't see *your* husband."

The other woman turned red. Blotches spread across her neck and chest. Seeing Conley approach, she spat, "Don't judge me, missy. You seem to be having a fling of your own."

Jo reached a hand toward Conley. "This is my new husband, Conley. Conley, Meredith, gossip of Prestige."

Meredith huffed, spun on her heel, and stalked away. Conley's amused glance rested on Jo. "Our room is right here." He held up a small paper bag. "I got you some bubble bath and aspirin. Maybe it will help your headache." He offered a hand to assist her off the bike.

"That woman will have it all over town by morning that we've arrived."

"So? Everyone will find out shortly anyway." He unlocked the door and ushered her inside. "Have a seat while I run your bath."

The room was one of the cleaner ones they'd spent the night in. Decorated in muted colors of mauve, rose, and mint green, it was designed to comfort and relax. Floral prints adorned walls of pale rose paint. Jo sniffed. No mildew or other offensive odors assaulted her. The air conditioner hummed softly in the background. She smiled and fell into one of the soft, stuffed chairs, and rested her head in her hands.

"Come on, sweetheart." Conley held out a hand

holding two aspirins and a glass of water.

She downed the white tablets and grasped his hand before allowing him to lead her to the restroom. Tears sprang to her eyes. A tub of fragrant bubbles awaited her. A scented candle rested on the side of the tub, and a plastic goblet of amber liquid sparkled next to it. "Champagne?"

Conley gave her a crooked smile. "Non-alcoholic cider. Prestige is a dry county, I found out."

"Why are you so good to me?"

"Because you deserve it. Hasn't anyone been nice to you before?"

"Not without wanting something in return. What do *you* want, Conley?" It wasn't possible he only wanted to help her. No man looked at a woman like that. None she'd ever met, anyway. No, there was something about Conley Hook that got under a person's skin.

"Nothing." He bent and placed a kiss on her forehead. "Enjoy your bath. Hope your head feels better." With those words, he stepped back and closed the door.

She dropped her clothes to the floor and stepped into the hot water. She gasped at the heat before gingerly lowering herself until the only part of her body not submerged was her head. The door opened just enough for Conley's arm to appear. He dropped a tee shirt on the counter.

"Something clean for you to sleep in." The door closed.

Tears fell anew. If someone would have asked her why she cried, she wasn't sure she'd be able to answer. The realization of no one treating her as if she were precious before rose up and slapped her. Was it Conley's God who made him so kind? The god her parents had shown her was one of rules and obedience. Not love. She prayed, but never felt like God listened.

She stayed in the tub until the water grew cool and goose bumps broke out on her flesh. Rising from the now bubble-less tub, she dried off on one of the thick towels and donned the tee shirt. She sniffed. It might be clean, but it smelled of the musky male scent she'd come to associate with Conley. Smiling, she opened the door.

The room lay in shadows. Conley had hung their new clothes on the clothing rack and now slept on the only bed. The television played with the sound muted.

Jo walked over and pressed the power button. She turned back toward the bed when Conley stirred. He remained asleep and she joined him, sliding carefully onto the vacant side of the bed, not wanting to wake him.

The ringing of the phone startled her awake. She jerked. Reaching blindly for the receiver, she knocked it to the floor.

"What?" Conley rolled over, eyes open.

"I'll get it. Go back to sleep." She fumbled on the floor until she found the cord and pulled the phone toward her. "Hello?"

"Jocelyn."

"Mother." Jo sat up and scooted back against the headboard. "How did you find us?"

Her mother sighed. "There's one hotel in town. We hired the man you're with so your father and I are familiar with his name. Is it true you actually married him? This is very disturbing news, Jocelyn."

"What time is it?"

"Don't change the subject. Answer the question."

Jo reached up and rubbed the back of her neck. "Yes, Mother, I did."

"What were you thinking? That man is not our type of people. I'll never be able to show my face in this town again."

The twitching in her eye returned. "Don't be so dramatic. Once I have Alex, I'll be gone. Your precious reputation will still be intact."

Conley sat up and removed her hand from her neck, replacing it with his. His strong fingers kneaded her tense shoulders, moving from the base of her skull and down. She moaned with the pleasure of it.

"Jocelyn? What are you doing?"

"Talking to you, but I'm finished. I'll see you in the morning." She replaced the phone in its cradle, as Conley dropped his hands.

"You okay?" He plopped onto his side.

"I'm fine." She slid until she laid on her side facing him. "Are you nervous at all?"

"About what? I've met your parents before."

"Not as my husband."

He ran his hand through his hair then rolled to his

111

back. "You're right, but I think I'll manage."

"Why are you always so sure?"

His eyes rolled to meet her gaze. "Why wouldn't I be? I'm comfortable with who I am. I eat with my mouth closed, put my pants on one leg at a time, and take showers regularly." He rolled back over and propped himself on one elbow. "They're only people, Jo. Like you and I. They cry when sad, and they bleed when cut. Just flesh and blood people."

There was just enough light filtering in the room for Jo to see his features. The straight Roman nose, high forehead, tousled curl that fell forward over one eye that looked dark and shining in the dimness. Her gaze fell to his mouth and focused on the smile that featured a dimple at the corner. The cut on his chin had scabbed over, leaving a black line in his ever-present stubble. Conley always looked like he needed to shave.

She'd never noticed before how attractive he was. No wonder women stared when they saw him. Seeing his smile widen, she frowned. He knew it, too. He knew his power over women. Blake did, too, but with Conley it was different. He loves the attention, accepts it, and treats women as precious things. Things worthy of his admiration and respect. Blake treats them as objects. Things owed him.

"Your parents must have been something," she said.

"They were."

She raised a finger and flicked the curl out of his face. "You're so caring. The tattoos and funny-man attitude are misleading. They make you out to be a tough guy, but you're not."

"I am a tough guy."

"No, not really." Her words slurred with tiredness.

"Go back to sleep." Conley slid an arm under her neck and pulled her close.

*

Not a tough guy? He'd always thought of himself as such. Juvenile detention had only made him tougher, or so he'd thought. A slow smile spread across his face, and he tightened his hold on the woman beside him. She felt so good lying there. Faint snores emanated from her, and her breath tickled his chest. If that was all he would get from her, he was all right with it.

The phone woke them as the sun rose. Its rays streamed through the slit in the curtains. Jo grumbled beneath her breath.

Conley reached across her to answer the phone. "Hello."

"Let me speak with my wife."

"Well, hello Mr. Nielson, but I'm afraid she's my wife now."

A curse exploded through the line. Conley held the phone away from his ear. Jo grabbed it from him.

"What do you want, Blake? We just got in last night. Who told you we were here? Meredith? Still seeing her behind her husband's back?" Jo leaned into Conley. "Where's Alex? I want to talk to him. I need to know he's all right." Her trembling started as the wheezing began. Conley tightened his arms around her.

"We'll be staying at my parents...they'll have to accept him...it's only for a while." Her voice broke and Conley took the phone away from her.

"This conversation is finished, Mr. Nielson." He banged the phone into its cradle then held Jo from him at arms-length. "Go put on your self-confidence. I'll get dressed out here."

He riffled through the few clothes on the hangar and pulled out a pair of cream colored linen trousers and a sky blue gentleman's shirt. How'd she sneak this sissy thing in there? Frowning, he slid his arms into the cotton shirt and discovered he liked the feel of the cool fabric.

Once dressed, he stood before the mirror and searched his reflection. A stranger stared back. A well-dressed man in expensive clothes with too long hair. He flexed his arm, testing the pull on his wound. Not bad. Only a little painful. The shirt sleeves hid his tattoos. He laughed. The little sneak.

"You look nice."

Conley turned. Jo wore black, wide leg pants and a sleeveless turtleneck sweater in a warm coral color. She wore her long hair clipped back in gold barrettes.

She smiled up at him. "Casual, yet not too casual."

"I feel like I should be out playing golf." He laughed.

"Do you play golf?"

"Yes. I'm good, too." He stopped laughing. "Why?"

She shrugged. "My father may ask you to play. If he does, make sure you beat him. He judges a man by how

114

he plays, and my father is very good."

"Great." Conley spared one more glance into the mirror. "I'll forgo shaving. Fits my image of the idle playboy." He offered Jo his elbow. "Shall we?"

Jo's smile stretched from ear to ear when she spotted the taxi waiting for them. "Thank you. I dreaded arriving on the back of a motorcycle." He opened the door for her and stepped back. "Where are you going?"

"I'm riding the bike." He straddled the Harley and clipped on his helmet. "We can't leave it here. I'll follow you."

The drive through the tree shaded streets of Prestige filled Conley with a sense of peace. Only beauty reigned in this part of town, in its Victorian style homes, tall trees that formed a canopy over the street, muted children's laughter, and lawns dressed in a riot of early fall color.

No trash cans lined the sidewalk. No litter lay in the gutter. Lawns were green with the beginning growth of winter grass. Wealth oozed from the homes and expensive cars sitting in driveways.

Jo stood before one of the Victorians, staring up at its egg shell blue paint and white shutters. Her lips were compressed and a deep frown marred her brow. In the driveway sat a silver Mercedes and a black Volvo. She turned to Conley, eyes wide in her pale face. "Blake is here."

"I'll be with you the entire time, Jo. Right by your side." He took her hand in his, and squeezed. "I'm not going anywhere."

11

The music of Westminster chimes rang out when Jo pushed the doorbell. Within seconds, the double, glass-paned doors swung open. She and Conley were ushered into a spacious foyer.

"I'll let Mr. and Mrs. Woodward know you're here." The maid bobbed her head and disappeared through an archway to their left.

A padded bench sat against one wall and Jo marched to it, the heels of her boots clicking on the marble floor. She lowered herself to the cushions, popping back up immediately as her mother entered the room.

Her mother's hair was silver and styled into a fashionable bob. Grey slacks and a grey long sleeve sweater covered her willowy frame. She fingered the reading glasses hanging around her neck on a pearl strand. She acknowledged Conley's presence with a nod then focused her attention on Jo. "Jocelyn." Her fingers clicked along the pearl strand as if she were counting a rosary.

"Mother."

Sylvia Woodward compressed her lips, the only sign of her displeasure. "We have a predicament, Jocelyn."

"Hello to you, too."

Sylvia frowned and fiddled with her pearls. "We've planned a party for your return. Tonight, in fact. Invitations were sent out yesterday announcing the occasion. Unfortunately," she cast a glance at Conley before finishing. "Our guests are expecting you to be standing at Blake's side, not Mr. Hook's."

As if on cue, Blake and Jo's father joined Sylvia, and Conley stepped forward to place himself next to Jo.

"That was presumptuous of you." Jo stepped closer to Conley. Her arm brushed his and she drew upon his strength, firming her jaw and tilting her chin.

"We must keep up appearances. We can't have the neighbors talking."

"Talking! Mother, I've remarried and now I'm here to get my son."

"Jocelyn." Blake took a step forward, his voice low. Jo stepped back. "We all know your marriage is one of convenience. A childish act of you trying to get back at me for some imagined wrong." He held his hands out. "I love you. Come to your senses and come home where you belong."

She grabbed Conley's hand. "I am where I

belong." She reached up and pulled Conley's face to hers for a kiss. Her eyes cast a sideways glance toward those watching. The smile remained on Blake's face despite the growing coldness in his eyes. A shiver ran down Jo's spine, and she kept her hold of Conley's hand.

"Enough of this," Jo's father spoke up. "There is a room ready for you upstairs. You and...your husband...may deposit your things there. The party begins at eight. It's formal." He took his wife's elbow and pulled her from the foyer.

Blake took another step forward and placed himself inches from Conley. The two men's gazes clashed, then Conley flashed his crooked smile. "Can I help you with something?"

"This isn't over Mr. Hook. Not by a long shot. I will have what is mine."

"And so will Jo." Conley placed his arm around her shoulders. "Sweetheart, why don't you run upstairs to our room, and I'll go outside and get our things."

She nodded numbly, not moving. The two men continued to stare each other down. Conley was taller than Blake by about three inches and broader through the shoulders. Blake was leaner. It was like a panther facing a lion.

Conley turned his attention to her and caressed her cheek. "I'll be right back. Go upstairs."

"I'll wait here." Her voice barely rose above a whisper. Her eyes flicked to her ex and then back to Conley.

He tossed a look over his shoulder as he strode out the door. Jo lowered her head and breathed a sigh of relief when he returned.

"A box?" Blake scoffed. "That contains all your things? Jocelyn, if only you'd come home. I've kept all of your belongings. They're waiting for you. Why must you deny yourself this way?"

"We left in kind of a hurry." Conley motioned with his head for Jo to precede him up the stairs. "Don't worry about us. We'll be fine."

When they reached the top, Jo glanced down the staircase to see Blake standing at the bottom, his features twisted. A muscle flicked in his jaw. Fear crawled up her. His mouth spread into a thin-lipped smile before he spun on his heel and stalked out of the house.

Jo opened the door to her old room. A four poster bed, covered with a gold duvet over burgundy sheets, took center stage in the middle of the room. A black tux, still in the plastic tailor's bag lay draped over the bedrail.

"Oh, goody." Conley sat the box at the foot of the bed, shoulders slumped. "My monkey suit is here." He went to open it, and Jo stopped him.

"You don't need to do that. The maid will..."

The young woman who had let them into the house entered the room. Without a word, she took the box and disappeared into a large walk-in closet.

"I'm an idiot." Jo fell across the bed. The satin duvet cover, cool under her cheek, smelled fresh and clean.

"How so?" Conley sat next to her.

"I freeze when Blake's around. Completely freeze. It's like I don't have a mind of my own." She kicked her feet, banging them against the bed.

He patted her back. "You're fine. Getting stronger all the time." He rose from the bed. "Besides, the guys a freak. He even scares me. Looking into his dark eyes is like staring down a shark. Lifeless."

Jo giggled and rolled over. She remained silent for a moment until the maid left, then added. "He does remind one of a shark. A cold fish with no soul." A sharp pain in her gut sobered her instantly. "A shark who has my son."

"We'll get Alex back."

"Let's go walk by his place. Maybe I'll see my son." She bounded from the bed. "We've got plenty of time before the party."

They made the walk in companionable silence, Jo lost in her thoughts, their gait slow and easy. A slight breeze blew, carrying with it an autumn nip. Brightly colored leaves rained down around them, carpeting the sidewalk. Jo sniffed. A fireplace burned, bringing to mind childhood memories of popcorn and marshmallows at her grandmother's house. Somewhere, a lawnmower roared, its sound muffled by distance. Conley took Jo's hand in his, lightly swinging their arms back and forth.

His hands were warm and calloused, completely engulfing Jo's smaller one, and filled her with a sense of safety. She tightened her pressure on his hand and received a small squeeze in return.

Blake's home sat back from the street on a wide, sloping lawn. A circular driveway wound around a marble fountain, bordered by flower beds. The red-brick mansion towered above the other homes on the street.

"Wow." Conley stopped at the edge of the driveway.

"Yeah." Jo slid her arm around his. She shivered in the cool air and pressed closer.

"It's huge. Why is it so much bigger than the other houses?"

"Blake bought two houses and lots on each side of this one, tore them down, and built this monstrosity."

"Let's go." Conley put a hand over the hand Jo held in the crook of his arm and marched toward the house.

"What if Blake sees us?"

"What if he does?"

With each step closer, Jo's heartbeat quickened. She swallowed against the lump in her throat and clutched Conley's arm tighter. "Alex."

Her son peered down from a second story building. The palms of his hands were flat against the glass and his lips moved as if he called to her. She stretched a trembling hand toward him.

Alex slapped his hands on the window, his mouth open wide. He banged against the glass.

Pulling her hand free of Conley's, Jo sprinted up the stairs and onto the porch. She tried the door handle and found it locked. With doubled fists, she pounded on the door, her breath coming fast. "Blake!"

She drew back a foot and kicked through the stained glass of the narrow window beside the door. Her leg screamed in pain. Blood trickled down her calf and into her boot. Alarms went off, reverberating inside her skull.

Conley grabbed her arms from behind and pulled her away.

"Let go of me. Alex! Blake!" She turned and landed a swift kick on Conley's shin.

"Stop it, Jo." He shook her. "Come on."

She pulled free again and hurled herself at the door. Conley picked her up and flung her across his shoulder. He hastened down the drive and into the street.

Jo kicked and screamed, pounding against his back. "Let me go. Please. Alex needs me."

"Listen to me." He set her on her feet and held her at arm's length. He stabbed her with his intense blue gaze. "You cannot break into Blake's house. Alex looks fine. Frightened, maybe, but unharmed. Now he knows you're here. That you're coming for him."

Her chest heaved as she fought to catch her breath. Conley's words slowly registered in her head. She nodded then glanced once more toward the house.

A young woman stood on the porch staring in their direction. The wind lifted the girl's dark tresses, flirting with them, blowing them across her face and then away. Jo's first thought was that Blake had hired a new maid, but then she noticed the red dress and high heels. Who was this girl?

"Do you know her?" Conley's voice cut through her thoughts. "She favors you."

She shook her head.

"Come on. Let's go get ready for the party." He took her by the arm and dragged her away.

Jo looked back once more. At the girl on the porch and then up at her son's face, framed in the window.

*

"Go on downstairs," Jo called from the closet. "I'll meet you in a few minutes."

Conley straightened the bow tie on his tux. "All right." He stared into the mirror. The pomade he'd used darkened his hair and tamed his curls. "I look like a big gorilla with yellow hair."

"What?"

"Nothing. I'll see you downstairs."

Soft music drifted up the stairs to greet him as he exited their room. He glanced upward looking for speakers. He shrugged, not locating any, and headed downstairs. A maid, decked out in black, complete with the white apron and cap, met him at the bottom.

"Please follow me, Mr. Hook."

He let her lead the way behind swinging oak doors and discovered the reason for no speakers. Conley stepped into a small ballroom with highly polished oak floors, crystal chandeliers, and a four-man orchestra. A large stone fireplace took center of attention along one wall. Opposite, were French doors leading to a flagstone terrace. He tugged at the bottom of his jacket and stepped forward.

"One moment, please," the maid stopped him. "I'll announce you. If you'd like to wait for Mrs. Hook…"

"No, that's all right. I'll go on in." *I couldn't live like this on a permanent basis. No privacy.*

Jo's parents stood near the dessert buffet, both dressed in black, oozing wealth and seemed deep in conversation with Blake. Conley felt a moment's gratitude to Jo for insisting he purchase the tuxedo he wore.

Meredith, the woman he'd seen Jo speaking to at the hotel, stood with cocked hip near the fireplace. One finely tweezed eyebrow arched in his direction. She, too, was dressed, barely, in black. The front of the dress plunged in a narrow v to her waist and Conley was sure the back did too. A slit rose from toe to knee. Blood red lips parted into a smile as his eyes lingered. He shrugged and turned away.

He continued to survey the room. Women, resplendent in costly gowns and sparkling jewels, hung on the arms of tuxedoed men. A light fragrance of pine drifted through the open doors and across the room, mingling with the sweet scent of the varied desserts.

Nodding toward Jo's parents, Conley stepped outside onto the terrace. Carefully placed lanterns marked the way down the flagstone path winding across closely manicured lawns. Muted conversations floated across the grounds from gazebos and hidden benches. The temperature dropped with the night's falling. He welcomed the chill in the air as he tugged at his tie. Sighing, he turned and reentered the room.

His heart stopped when he spotted Jo standing in the doorway. She'd swept her hair up, allowing a few curls to trail down, drawing the observer's eyes to her own. The burgundy wine colored dress skimmed her curves, falling just to the tips of the gold sandals on her feet and trailing behind her in a small train. The neckline hung in graceful folds of fabric. Her arms were bare. She smiled, and he stepped forward to greet her.

Blake was quicker and slid an arm around Jo's waist. "You look beautiful, Jocelyn."

She slid from his grasp. "Thank you."

"You look gorgeous. And you smell nice." Conley stepped between her and Blake. "I believe this is my dance." He led her to the center of the room.

"No one's dancing." Jo glanced around the room.

"We'll start." He placed his hands lightly on her waist, discovering the back of the dress draped to her waist, and led her to the music of the orchestra. For the first time in his life, he thanked his parents for the dance lessons they'd insisted he take.

Blake stood mere feet from them, his features looking like they were cast in stone. He raised his chin and strode toward Meredith. He pulled her close.

"Everyone is staring, Conley." Jo's brow

wrinkled, and he smoothed it with his finger.

"Then let's give them something to stare at." He dipped her low and bent to kiss her. His lips lingered on hers. Her face flushed when he raised her.

Blake swept his partner closer. "Stop mauling my wife."

"You, Mr. Nielson, are confused." Conley twirled Jo away. "She's my wife now."

"I will kill you," Blake hissed.

"Threat?" His voice lowered and, with blood boiling, he stared the other man down. "That would be a pity. Kill a man on his honeymoon? Where's your heart?"

"It's a promise." Blake stormed away, leaving a stunned Meredith standing in the middle of the floor with her mouth hanging open.

"You shouldn't have done that." Jo tucked a stray curl back up into her French twist. "Blake is not a man to be trifled with."

Conley planted a kiss on her forehead. "Neither am I." He crooked an arm, offering it to her. "Shall we eat?"

Out of some ridiculous purpose only they were aware of, Jo's parents seated Blake directly across the table from Conley and Jo. Every minuscule sound of fork against plate or sound of the man's glass being set on the table, grated on Conley's nerves.

He squinted at them over the top of his glass, his expression coldly neutral. He raised his goblet in a toast. "To the happy couple."

Jo's hand shook. Her fork clattered against the china, and Conley placed his hand over hers. His gaze never left Blake's. "Shark eyes," he whispered to Jo from the corner of his mouth. A nervous giggle escaped her, and she lifted her napkin to her mouth.

Meredith, sitting next to whom Conley assumed was her husband, cast looks between Blake and them. Occasionally, she peered at Blake with what Conley could only call 'hungry eyes'. The woman's husband seemed oblivious to the drama being played out around him.

Interesting party. Conley lowered his eyes and cut into his steak. Maybe once he got Jo away from the Woodward family circus, Meredith could become Blake's new possession. She looked willing to leave her husband fast enough.

When Jo's parents rose from their prospective ends of the table, their daughter did likewise, signaling to the guests it was permissible to move back into the ballroom.

"Walk with me." Conley placed a hand lightly on Jo's waist, her back warm against the palm of his hand.

They wove their way between dancing couples and out onto the terrace. Jo stepped down and onto the pathway. She cast a glance over her shoulder. "Want to get away from everyone?"

"Yes. That's the best thing I've heard all evening."

She led him to the right and down a path which seemed to disappear in front of a wall of trailing ivy. Jo glanced over her shoulder again, winked...and disappeared. Conley laughed and ducked around the hedge, ready for a bit of flirtation.

Jo's scream spurred him into a run.

12

Conley thrust aside overhanging ivy and bolted into a private garden. Moonlight streamed down, illuminating the enclosed area. Jo stood before the entrance to a white lattice work gazebo. Her hands covered her face.

She screamed again. Her voice ripped through the night. She whirled when he placed a hand on her shoulder.

"Shhh. It's me." He stepped forward and wrapped his arms around her. Conley rubbed her back and peered over the top of her head.

A young girl lay on the floor of the gazebo. The white gown she wore was splattered by blood. The slice in her neck appeared black in the light of the moon. Her eyes stared sightlessly up at them. Raven tresses fanned around her head. Conley wrinkled his nose against the rusty metallic smell of blood. The cloying scent of late blooming flowers mixed with the odor.

"It's the girl from Blake's house." Jo's words were muffled in Conley's chest.

Footsteps pounded from the other side of the wall. Inquiring voices rose and fell, questioning as they tried to discover the source of the scream. Harold Woodward burst through the foliage and stumbled into the garden, followed closely by Blake.

Harold stopped short, eyes wide behind his spectacles. "What...who?"

"Who is that?" Blake's words hung heavy in the air. "What happened?"

Jo raised her head. "You know who she is. Conley and I saw her at your house earlier today."

"We don't know what happened." Conley's finger traced the path of Jo's tears, wiping them from her face, before he turned to Blake. "Maybe you can tell us."

He shook his head. "Impossible. I've never seen that girl before."

"She was there, Nielson." He set Jo away from him and shrugged out of his jacket. He laid the jacket over the dead girl's face to hide her from prying eyes as people crowded around them. It was then he noticed her right index finger was missing. It had been severed at the knuckle. He placed the sleeve of his jacket so it covered her hand. "She was standing on your front porch decked out in a red dress."

"What are you implying?" Blake clenched his fists at his side. "Are you insinuating I had something to do with this girl's death?"

"I'm not insinuating anything."

"Stop it. Please." Jo sank to the concrete bench beside the gazebo. "The girl is dead. Let's not fight over where she was or wasn't."

"I'll phone the police." Harold turned and ushered the other guests from the garden. "I'll have to tell, Sylvia, too. She'll be curious … and disturbed."

Conley spared the man a glance and his eyebrows rose. *Curious and disturbed?*

Blake stepped forward. He planted his feet in the fallen leaves covering the ground. He stood close enough Conley could see the moon reflected in the man's dark eyes and smell the sweet fruity scent of the wine he'd drunk. "What were you doing at my house?"

"Taking a walk. Why? Worried?"

"I've nothing to be *worried* about."

"Really?" Conley's attention was diverted by the squeaks coming from Jo with each breath she took. He slid his hand into his pocket and pulled out her inhaler.

"Thank you. How did..?"

He sat next to her on the bench. "I knew you'd be stressed with your parents and ex-husband. Thought it better to be prepared. You really need to get into the habit of carrying it with you, although that dress doesn't leave many places to stash it." He placed an arm around her shoulders when she trembled. "Why don't you go in the house?"

She shook her head and administered a puff, visibly relaxing. "I want to stay with you."

"Don't ignore me, Hook." Blake pushed Conley with the palm of his hand. The shove caught him in the shoulder.

Conley leaned back before catching his balance and lunging to his feet. "Don't touch me again."

Blake pushed him again. "What are you going to do about it? Steal my car? I checked your rap sheet. You're a petty con. Worthless. That tux you're wearing is worth more than you are." His gaze rested on the jacket covering the girl's body. "Or it was."

Red hot anger rose in Conley. A scarlet haze spread across his mind, and he dug his fingernails into his palms as he doubled his hands into fists. "You need to walk away now, Nielson."

The other man scoffed. "I'm not afraid of you."

"Turn…and…walk…away." Conley's face heated.

Blake laughed. The sound loud in the still night air.

The contact of his right fist smashing against Blake's teeth, scraping his knuckles, surprised Conley. He'd swung before thinking, pulling back when the other man fell to the ground.

"I'll kill you for that." Blake pushed to his feet. He wiped his split lip on the back of his hand.

"You can try."

"No one touches me." He lunged to his feet and barreled into Conley.

Conley wrapped his arms around the man's middle, heaved him off his feet and slammed him to the ground. Blake grunted, cursing. Conley bounced lightly back and forth. He balanced on the balls of his feet and raised his fists in a defensive position.

"You..." Blake shoved against the bench and rose to his feet.

The arrival of two police officers interrupted them and Conley stepped back to take his place beside Jo.

She sat rigid, silent. Tears ran steadily down her cheeks. She stared straight ahead, not acknowledging when he placed his hand over the ones she'd clinched in her lap. Her hands were cold beneath his. He rubbed them, trying to instill some of his body warmth.

The older of the officers, a stout man of approximately fifty with salt and pepper hair, shook Blake's hand before standing in front of Jo. "Mrs. Nielson?" He held a clipboard with a pad of paper in one hand.

"It's Mrs. Hook," Conley corrected, his eyes not leaving Jo's white face.

"And you are?"

"Mr. Hook, her husband."

The officer was visibly confused and glanced from Conley to Blake and back to Jo. "I was under the impression..."

"Everyone is." Conley closed his eyes and scratched his forehead. "We're newlyweds. Married on the way out here."

"Okay." The officer nodded and wrote on his pad. "I'm Officer Settler and this is my partner Downs. Mrs. Hook, I was told you found the body?"

"Yes."

The officer had to lean close to hear her. Her eyes flicked to Downs who lifted the jacket from the girl's face. She lowered her head and turned away.

"The body is exactly as we found it." Conley pulled Jo's tense body closer. "Except for the jacket, which is mine."

"Any idea of who she is?"

Conley looked at Blake, who answered, "We've no idea, Officer. She's a stranger."

"Anyone see her at the party?"

"No."

The officer's eyes raked the garden. "Any idea of how she got onto the grounds?"

"There are a million ways. She could have walked on the property while we were eating dinner and no one would have been the wiser." Blake pulled a handkerchief from his pocket and wiped his brow.

"How'd you get the cut on your lip?"

"I tripped running in here after my wife…ex-wife screamed." Blake touched his lip with his index finger. "Look Officer Settler, we're tired, and it's been a traumatic evening for everyone. Take the girl and call it a night."

"Once we've interviewed everyone, we'll be on our way." The officer turned to Conley. "I hope you don't have plans on leaving town, Mr. Hook."

Conley shook his head and smirked. Once they punched his name into their computers, there'd be no question of them allowing him to leave.

The play between Blake and the officer kept Conley riveted. It was obvious by Blake's smile, it was an act. The officer knew Blake and knew him well. For Conley to speak up and contradict this man who appeared so highly favored in Prestige would only serve to put more suspicion on himself. He ran his hands up and down Jo's icy arms. Her flesh was pimpled with goose bumps.

She placed her head on his shoulder.

*

Unhooking the shoulder clasp of her gown, Jo allowed the gown to float to a silky puddle at her feet. She stepped out of it and into a tub of hot water, fragrant with a musky scented bubble bath. Candles flickered along the window sill, bathing the room in a comforting glow.

She sighed deeply and slid until her head and body were submerged. She only wanted to erase the events of the evening. Her body tingled as it adjusted to the warmer temperature. The images of the dead girl played in a never-ending circle through her mind. First in the red dress she'd worn at Blake's, her face tilted into the wind, then sprawled out in the white one, blood splattered. Eyes staring.

Terror for her son rose, breaking into her thoughts. She stayed submerged until her lungs screamed for air then she pushed herself to the surface. Why hadn't Conley mentioned to the police that they'd seen the girl at Blake's?

Her hand groped the edge of the tub, searching

for the dry towel she'd placed there. She brought it to her face and wiped the bubble bath from her eyes.

The bedroom door closed with a faint click. A shadow passed by the arch leading to the bath. She strained her neck to see more. "Conley?" She leaned further over the tub. The marble was cold against her stomach. Nothing moved, and she shrugged before settling back against the inflated bath pillow and closing her eyes.

An image of her Uncle Dave flashed to the front of her mind. She gasped. In her memory, he laughed and reached for her. More sounds issued from the bedroom. A muffled groan. A thud. Her eyes snapped open. The bedroom was dark. "Conley?" Her voice trembled and sounded hoarse to her ears. She wasn't alone with her bad memories.

She stood. Her body moved slow and heavy as if through thick mud. Bubbles slid down her body to rejoin those in the water. She picked up the towel and wrapped it around her as a breeze whipped past. The candles flickered, then blew out. The bathroom was plunged into darkness. Jo stepped forward and put her back to the wall. She froze as icy terror engulfed her.

Stealthy footsteps slid across the wooden floor. A groan issued from the far side of the room. Jo fought against her increasing panic and squelched the whimpers rising in her throat.

A man wearing a dark ski-mask darted around the corner. Jo slid sideways in an attempt to duck beneath his outstretched arm. A hand tangled in her hair.

He pulled her close and slammed her against the wall. Her head connected with the tiles. Her teeth clicked together. Bile rose and burned the back of her throat. She swallowed convulsively.

She kicked. Her knee connected with the man's inner thigh. He grunted and banged her head once more against the wall. Pinpricks of light swam before her eyes. She lashed out again. He back-handed her across the mouth.

Her lip split. Her mouth filled with the copper taste of blood. Where was Conley? Fear rose in her, filling her stomach and squeezing her heart in its iron fist. She increased her struggles, refusing to go down without a fight. The man's hands tightened on her shoulders. His fingers dug into her flesh, pushing against bone.

The towel fell to the floor, and Jo grappled desperately for it. Her assailant pinned her to the wall with his forearm across her throat, constricting her breathing. She wheezed. Her bronchial tubes seized closed.

She opened her mouth to scream and the man's other hand clamped over her mouth and nose cutting off her oxygen supply. With a whimper, her world went black.

She came to lying on the icy marble of the bathroom floor. She was curled into a fetal position and stared at the muddy boots of her attacker.

Hazel eyes stared through ski mask eyeholes at

her. Full lips pulled back into a sneer.

"What do you want?" Her voice shook as she struggled to a sitting position. Stabs of pain shot through her head. She put up a hand to discover a lump rising above her temple.

"There isn't time for what I want." He cackled. His eyes roved over her body. She reached for the towel and draped it across her.

"I've got a message for you from your husband." The man towered over her. "Go home now and end the pain. If you don't, others will suffer."

She shook. The shivers seemed hard enough to rattle her bones. "What did you do with my husband?"

"Killed him, I hope. I hit him hard enough to fell a horse." The man bent and pinched her face between his fingers. He bent low, drawing his tongue across her cheek. "It's a pity there's not more time." He tapped his hand against her cheek, and left.

"God, help me," she whispered.

She didn't know how long she lay there. A groan from the bedroom spurred her to action. She raised her head and hope bloomed within her. She planted her hands against the floor and pushed until she regained her footing.

Wrapping the towel around her, she firmly tucked the ends under and secured it. Another groan urged her to move faster. She flicked on the light and rushed across the room and into the closet.

Conley lay crumbled on the floor. Blood matted the hair on the back of his head. Jo knelt beside him and rolled him over. "Conley?" She patted his face and ran her gaze over him as she searched for other signs of injury.

His eyes flickered, blinked, and then focused on her face. "Are you all right?"

"Me?" A sob tore at her throat. "What about you? That man meant to kill you."

Conley's eyes closed. "I'm sure he did, but he failed. I'm a hard man to kill. What did he hit me with?"

Looking around the closet, Jo spotted her old wooden baseball bat. "A bat. You should be dead."

"I heard him and turned. Don't worry. God isn't finished with me yet." He put his elbows beneath him. "Help me up. We need to alert your parents."

She put her arms around him and let him use her as leverage. "We can't. My parents are involved in this."

"What?" He squinted.

"I'm remembering things, Conley. Horrible things. Things that happened to me as a child." She grunted under his weight. "Things about my uncle. There's too much showing up for my parents to not have been aware of what was going on."

She grabbed a robe from the foot of the bed then slid her arms into the soft silk of the sleeves. She untied the towel and let if fall to the floor. Tremors took control of her legs, and she dropped to the edge of the bed.

"What happened when I was unconscious?" He touched her arm, and she jerked away.

"Nothing."

"Jo," his voice pleaded with her.

"Nothing! He wouldn't dare. Blake would've killed him." She bolted upright. "That's when the rapes ended. Once I married Blake, no other man dared touch me."

"Look at me."   Tears welled in her eyes at the compassion in his voice. She could have drowned in the blue of eyes. "Was your uncle the only one?"

13

Why can't she just love me? I gave her everything-- my love, my support, my safety. Blake paced the room, from fireplace to window, from window to door. The heels of his shoes snapped against the wood of the floor. *I gave her son my name!*

He stopped and pinched the bridge of his nose between shaky fingers. His chest heaved. His breathing came heavy and fast.

A heavy knock on the door startled him and he jerked. "What?"

"It's me." The voice was deep and hoarse.

"Come in, then." Blake stepped behind his desk and plopped into the massive leather chair.

"It's done." The man stood before him.

"He's dead?" A slow smile spread across Blake's face. The pendulum on the grandfather clock seemed to tick quicker with expectancy, as if it too were waiting for the assailant's answer.

"I hit him with a baseball bat." The man pounded one fist into the palm of the other hand.

"And her?" Blake leaned forward. His elbows rested on the polished surface of the desk. "You didn't touch her?"

The man's eyes widened. "No...no, sir. She's fine. I left her in good health."

Blake studied the man's face. A crimson shade of fear crept up the man's neck and swept across his face. A fine sheen of perspiration dotted his upper lip and forehead. "You're lying."

"No...really...I left her alone. Just like you said." His thick tongue flicked across his lips. He swallowed. The Adam's apple in his throat bobbed.

Leaning back into his chair Blake steepled his fingers and rested them against his chin. "Mmm." He squinted. "I pray not--for your sake. With Hook dead, she will again belong to me. Move on to the next step in our plan."

"Yes, sir." The man took a deep breath, his words shaky. "Right away." He turned and scurried from the room. One beefy shoulder banged against the door frame as he rushed out. A landscape painting crashed to the floor.

Blake cackled and clapped his hands. *Soon, Jocelyn, my dear. Soon you will come crawling back to me and if that hired oaf has touched you...touched what is mine...He will join Hook in the land of the dead.*

The grandfather clock chimed one o'clock, and

Blake laughed again, the sound of it shrill and girlish in his ears. He lifted Jocelyn's portrait from his desk and stroked it with one gentle finger.

*

Jo lay next to Conley, separated by mere inches—and a mile. Her thoughts isolated her, casting her adrift on a solitary raft. Tears poured in a never-ending river down her cheeks and soaked into her hair and pillow.

Had she been passed around like a discarded toy? *Did* her parents know? Had they allowed it?

Waves of raw pain swept through her, and she trembled. Conley's hand grasped hers. He entangled her fingers with his.

Her throat ached from suppressing her sobs, and she yanked her hand free to beat her fists on the mattress. "How could they? How could they allow that to happen to me?" Her eyes narrowed. "And now they have my son and they expect me to go back to the arms of the man they chose for me?"

"Honey." Conley reached for her.

Jo rolled away and dashed from the bed. She rushed across the room and yanked the bedroom door open. She tossed a glance over her shoulder at an astonished Conley who stared wide-eyed after her. "I won't allow it. I won't."

"Jo." Conley sat up then fell back onto the pillows, an arm thrown across his face. "Wait."

"Stay there. I'm not leaving the house." She grabbed her robe and donned it over her nightgown.

She marched past a wide-eyed servant, arms laden

with plush towels, who bustled around preparing the house for another day. Without knocking, Jo burst into her parent's room.

Harold and Sylvia sprang upright from a massive sleigh bed. Sylvia clutched the forest green silk sheets to her chest. "What is the meaning of this?" She glanced at the bedside clock. "It's 4:30 in the morning."

"I don't care what time it is, Mother." Four-thirty? How long had she been unconscious while that mad man stared at her body? She stood beside the bed and glared down at the older woman. Her eyes flicked to her father and back again to focus on her mother's face. "Are the two of you aware there was an intruder in the house?"

Harold blinked, reminding Jo oddly of an owl. "An intruder? Here? In our house?"

"Impossible." Sylvia let the sheets fall and swung her silk pajama clad legs over the side of the bed. Jo hopped back to avoid being kicked. "We have a state-of-the-art alarm system."

"Then someone *let* him in."

Harold groped his nightstand. His hand riffled through the discarded tissues and magazines. Locating his glasses, he placed them on his face. "Jocelyn, dear, are you sure? Couldn't you have been mistaken...dreaming?"

Her mouth fell open and she clamped it shut. "Of course I'm not mistaken. While I was bathing a few hours ago, a man entered our room, knocked my husband unconscious, and attacked me."

"Is Conley all right, dear?" Sylvia slipped her arms into a robe. Her emotionless voice showed no concern over his welfare.

"He probably has a concussion."

"Pity."

Jo placed her hands on her hips. "Excuse me?"

Her mother waved a hand in the air. "Nothing. I see there's no chance of our getting any sleep. Come on, Harold. We might as well go downstairs and get some coffee."

"That's it? Coffee?" Jo's voice rose. "That's all you have to say?"

Sylvia sighed. "Is the man still upstairs?"

"No."

"Then there's nothing more to be done."

"You knew about this. You've set the alarm every night for as long as I can remember. You didn't set it last night on purpose."

"Don't be silly. Why would your father put us in that type of danger? We just forgot in last night's horrific circumstances."

"That would be the time a person wouldn't forget." Fury and disbelief rose and threatened to choke her. Jo's hands trembled. "I think the two of you are in cahoots with Blake. You're trying to frighten me into going back with him." She plopped into an easy chair beside the bed and covered her face with her hands. "Well, I won't do it. I'm married to Conley now. I want my son so I can leave."

"You always were melodramatic. I'm convinced

you dreamed the whole thing up. Come on, Harold." Sylvia spun on her heel and marched out of the room.

Harold placed a hand on Jo's shoulder. "You've been under a lot of stress lately, dear."

She pulled away from his touch. "I didn't dream up the bruises, did I?" She pulled up the sleeve of her robe, revealing the deepening blue and purple marks.

"Does Conley hit you?" Harold's eyes were wide behind his glasses.

"I don't believe this." She frowned at her father's back as he followed his wife from the room. Were they really that cold? That cruel?

She stormed from the room and stomped back to her husband. He sat slumped on the edge of the bed. His shoulders hunched. Jo flicked on the light.

"They think I dreamed the whole thing up and that I'm covering up for the fact you beat me."

"Huh?" He squinted.

Jo paced the room. Her voice shook as she ground out the words. "I told them about our attacker. They said I dreamed it. At least that's the story they would tell Prestige's farce of a police department." She waved her arms and increased her pace. "Can you imagine? Then I showed my father my bruises and he asked me whether you beat me. I couldn't believe it. I wanted to strangle him. My mother was totally unaffected. Emotionless" At Conley's lack of response, she turned to stare at him. "Are you okay?"

"I need some aspirin."

"I'm so sorry." She rushed to the medicine cabinet

and took out a small bottle of aspirin. While she ranted and raved, the poor man suffered from a bash on his head. "You're injured and all I've done is grumble and complain about my own treatment." Next to the sink sat a small crystal glass and decanter. Jo filled the glass with water from the decanter. She spilled some of the liquid in her haste.

"Thanks." He gulped three of the white tablets and chased them down with the water.

"Let me look at your head."

Conley turned, allowing her access to the gash at the base of his skull. He exhaled in a hiss as her fingers probed.

"You need stitches."

"Forget it. Just clean it with a rag. I'll be fine. It's not the first time I've been beaten over the head. Probably won't be the last." He groaned and fell back onto the bed.

Jo retrieved a snow white wash cloth from under the bathroom sink and soaked it with hot water. After wringing out the excess, she perched on the side of the bed. "Roll over."

"You're killing me."

"Stop whining."

He rolled over and clutched one of the pillows beneath him. The muscles in his back quivered as she wiped at the wound. Once finished, she patted him between the shoulder blades and rose.

"I'm getting dressed. I can't sleep." She ducked back into the closet.

"Guess I won't sleep either. Were they surprised about our attacker?"

"No. Not in the slightest." She poked her head around the door jamb. "My father kind of acted like it…maybe, but I don't think he was." She ducked back into the closet and pulled on a pair of jeans and a sweater.

The baseball bat poked out from under a pair of discarded pants. Jo's breath hitched as she bent to pick it up. A small trace of blood and blond hair stuck to one side. She thought of fingerprints and quickly dropped it, grimacing. She'd take it to the police station later. Not that it would matter much.

The warm, comforting smell of fresh roasted coffee greeted her and Conley before they entered the kitchen. She placed a hand on his arm, stepped through the arched doorway into the kitchen—and froze. Blake smiled at her from the table where he sat sipping coffee with her parents.

"Heard you had an intruder." He lifted the steaming mug to his smiling mouth. "Or was it a little domestic dispute?"

Conley chose a chair across the table from Blake and sat. He leaned his elbow on the tabletop and supported his head in his hand. "A lover's spat, actually."

Blake's eyes darkened and a flush rose in his cheeks. He swiveled his head and focused his gaze on Jo. She took a deep breath, squared her shoulders, and stood her ground. She wouldn't cower for him anymore.

"Just a misunderstanding," she said, standing behind Conley. She placed her hands on his shoulders and kneaded the taut muscles. "But we've made up."

Coffee sloshed over the top of Blake's mug as his hand shook. He crashed the mug down on the table, cracking the porcelain. A bead of coffee leaked through, hanging on to the side of the mug. Blake stood. "Well, I've got a busy day ahead of me." He avoided Jo's eyes, directing his words to her parents. "I'll talk to you later."

"I'll walk you out." Harold rose from his chair. Throwing a warning look toward his daughter, he followed Blake out the door.

She took the chair he vacated and reached for her own cup of coffee. She pulled the mug to her nose and breathed in the aroma. She closed her eyes with the pleasure of it.

"Changed your story, didn't you?" Sylvia's chair scraped across the marble floor.

"You didn't believe me." Jo opened her eyes.

"It's only that…" Her mother was interrupted by the maid's arrival. The young lady carried a small cardboard box.

"This is for Mrs. Hook," the girl said, keeping her eyes down.

"For me?" Jo took the box and shook it.

"Don't." Conley roused enough to take the box from her. "Step back." He sniffed the box and set it carefully on the table.

"Why? What are you afraid of?"

"It could be anything. With this group of nutcases,

who knows?" He withdrew a small folding knife from his pocket and cut through the tape holding the top flaps closed.

Jo pressed close, leaning around his shoulder. Inside the box sat a small, rectangular box of the type jewelers' used for necklaces.

Withdrawing it, Conley removed the lid. Jo gasped. Inside, nestled on white tissue paper with a red bow tied around the stub, was a severed finger. Complete with a red sculptured fingernail.

14

"He's still alive, you imbecile." Blake slammed the phone into its cradle, missed, and slammed it again. He grabbed the glass paperweight from his desk and hurled it through the plate glass window of his office. He snatched a brass lamp and sent it flying after the paperweight. Figurines and books were tossed with increasing fury through the shattered window.

Blake stood in the middle of the room, breathless, hands clenched into fists at his side. His eyes burned. He scanned the walls. There was nothing left small enough to throw. The phone rang, and he lifted the phone receiver.

"You're growing careless, Blake. Killing Hook couldn't have been any easier. We handed him to you."

"I hired someone. Next time I'll do it myself." He fell into his chair.

"Uhmmhmm." The clicking of a ballpoint pen

sounded in Blake's ear.

"I will." His stomach churned. Acid rose into his esophagus.

"You're obsessed with ..."

"She's my wife!" Blake spun around in his chair and stared out the shattered window. A sparrow landed on the windowsill. Blake held the phone in place on his shoulder. Positioning his fingers in the shape of a gun, he pointed them at the bird.

"And I'll help you get her back. Focus." Click.

Blake cursed and gawked at the receiver. It occurred to him to yank the phone from the wall. Instead, he placed it very carefully into its cradle and went to stand before the window. He folded his hands behind his back and stared down into the lush lawn below him. Alex played with a soccer ball, kicking it back and forth under the subtle scrutiny of his nanny.

Maybe I could expend some of my angry energy on her? Looking down into the woman's plain face and rounded figure hidden under layers of nondescript clothing, he shook his head. I'd only have to hire another woman who follows orders and knows how to keep her mouth shut.

*

The throbbing in his head increased as Conley stared down at the severed finger. "It's the dead girl's from last night. It turned up quicker than I thought."

"You knew about this?" Jo stared at him.

"Only that she was missing a finger."

Sylvia stood behind him, peering over his shoulder.

"Get that thing out of my kitchen."

Eyes widening, Jo leaned against the wall. "What a horrible thing to say. Even for you, Mother. A girl has been murdered."

Sylvia fingered the pearls around her neck. "That...thing won't help the girl any."

"It's evidence, Mrs. Woodward. We'll take it, and the bat upstairs, to the police."

"I'll get the bat." Jo pushed away from the wall.

Conley watched Jo leave the room before turning to her mother. He stared until Sylvia turned away. Her fingers increased their pace up and down the strand around her neck. "If you know anything about the man who attacked us last night, now is the time to tell me."

"I don't know what you're talking about." Her hand shook as she spooned a bit of sugar into her coffee.

"I think you do." Conley reached for a cup of his own. He poured it full of the still warm coffee.

The woman's face drained of color and her constantly moving hand stilled.

"Last night your husband didn't set the alarm. An intruder entered our room and attacked us. Before that, a young girl was brutally murdered in your garden." He spooned a teaspoon of sugar into his cup. "You're mighty calm during all this. Most people would be afraid, nervous, anxious. Pick your adjective."

"What are you insinuating?" Her hoarse voice barely reached across the table.

"Nothing." Conley raised his head and grinned. Planting the palms of his hands on the table, he pushed himself to his feet. "Oh, by the way, you might be interested to know your daughter is remembering...things from her past."

Sylvia's lips formed an O. Her eyes mimicked the shape. A small gasp of breath escaped her.

"It's gone." Jo burst into the kitchen and leaned, breathless, against the door frame. "Someone removed the bat from our closet."

Conley turned to Sylvia. Her shoulders relaxed beneath the cashmere sweater she wore.

"What bat?" she asked.

"The bat someone used to bash Conley with."

"Well, we've still got the finger." Conley tucked the box beneath his arm, took Jo by the elbow, and turned her toward the front door. "Later, Mrs. Woodward. I enjoyed our little chat." He swiped a sweater from the coat tree in the foyer and handed it to Jo.

"Where are we going?" She snatched a set of keys from a small tray and scurried to keep up with him.

"The police station."

"Here." She tossed him the keys. "We'll take the Mercedes. You drive."

"Great!"

Jo punched in the garage door code and stepped back as the door rose. Parked neatly between an SUV and a Rolls Royce sat a black Mercedes.

"Sweet." Conley caressed the car as he walked to the driver's side door. "What a beautiful car."

"It was...is mine." Jo's smile shone across the hood.

His grin broadened. "Even sweeter."

With a feeling of almost reverence, Conley opened the door and slid inside. Inhaling broadly, he drew in the scent of leather. He passed his hand over the buttery soft skin of the seats. "I think I've died and gone to heaven."

Jo giggled, closing the passenger door. "It's yours."

"What?" His head whipped to face her. His smile faded.

"It's yours. I'm giving it to you."

"I can't take this."

"Why not? You're my husband. I can give you anything I want." Her brows drew together in a scowl.

"Jo." Conley shook his head. "You know we don't have a typical marriage." *Although I would love for it to be*. "What applies to others doesn't apply to us."

She turned in her seat to face him. "You've done so much for me. A complete stranger to you. You've risked everything for me and my son. This is my thanks. It is *very* small in comparison." Jo flopped back against the seat and folded her arms across her chest. "Are we going?"

Conley sighed and turned the key in the ignition. The engine hummed to life and the smile returned to his face. "Okay, I accept the car. Thank you." With a huff she settled deeper into the seat.

The car purred down the streets of Prestige, and Conley completely forgot his aching head. Occasionally, he'd glance over at Jo, but even her stoic silence couldn't dampen his mood.

The sight of the white box on the dashboard

threatened to dispel his feeling of joy, though. He removed it and tucked it out of sight in the glove compartment. He gave Jo a lopsided grin. She huffed again and turned her head.

"I said I was sorry. I love the car, Jo. Why are you mad?"

 "Turn right at the next stop sign."

He sighed and turned the wheel.

*

It had never occurred to Jo that Conley would be reluctant to accept the car as a gift. His reluctance to do so reminded her of her own misgivings to accept *his* help. The thought clinched her heart in a vise. If she hadn't accepted his help, where would she be now?

The police station came in view, and she turned to Conley. His hair was mussed from the open window. The sun through the open sun-roof of the car highlighted the blond curls falling around his face. He reminded her of a warrior angel, sent from heaven, clad in a tight blue tee shirt and jeans. All he lacked was the halo.

If she looked hard enough, she'd probably find it. He still grinned, his pleasure aglow on his face, and she fought not to return the smile. She shook her head and rolled her eyes. He was like a little boy with a new toy. "Apology accepted," she mumbled. "How's your head?"

"My what?"

"Exactly." She opened her door and slid from her seat before he'd cut the ignition.

He popped the glove compartment, grabbed the box, and sprang from the car. "Jo, wait up. I don't like police stations."

She whipped around, hand on hip. This time she couldn't resist an answering smile. "This time you need my help?"

"Got ya." Conley reached around her and opened the door. Her body tingled where his shoulder brushed hers, and her face heated.

They entered a small room with a glass enclosed cubicle in one corner. Black letters painted on the door read Chief of Police. In the center of the room, were two other police officers sitting behind battered metal desks. Meredith sat behind a low counter, thumbing through a magazine.

"Yes?" She didn't look up.

"We'd like to see the chief, please." The other woman's head shot up, connecting with Jo's. *How many times am I going to run into her? The hotel, the party, now here*.

The receptionist tossed a glance over her shoulder. "He's busy."

"He doesn't look busy." The chief stared at Jo through the glass before quickly ducking his head.

"Well, he is." Meredith returned her attention to the magazine on her desk.

"Too busy to see this?" Conley opened the white box and set it in front of her.

Meredith gasped and rolled back in her chair. She covered her mouth with one hand and bolted from her chair.

"Guess we'll have to show ourselves back." He snatched the box and pushed aside a swinging gate, then ushered Jo across the black and white tiled floor ahead of him.

The chief watched them come, not moving from his desk, a frown on his broad face. The fifty something-year-old man looked vaguely familiar to Jo. Her flesh crawled. Did she remember him from her childhood or sometime more recently? Was this always going to be the case when she saw a man who triggered particles of memory? She stepped back against the safety of Conley.

He steadied her with his hands and whispered, "It's all right. I'm right here."

Immediately her heart steadied. "A man attacked us last night." Her eyes flicked to the name plate on his desk. "Officer Logan. My husband was knocked unconscious. I was strangled until I passed out."

Logan folded his hands across his huge paunch of a stomach and leaned back in his chair. "Was this before or after the girl's murder?"

Jo frowned. "What difference does that make?"

Officer Logan's chair banged forward, and he propped his elbows on his desk. "Why are you waiting until now to report an assault, Mrs. Nielson?"

"It's Mrs. Hook." Conley rolled a chair behind her, and she fell into it.

"Mrs. Hook." Logan pinched the bridge of his

nose. "Your father already called me this morning. We're looking into it."

"Any progress on the dead girl?" Conley pulled up another chair.

Logan shook his head. "Nothing. No one knows her or where she came from."

"This was delivered to the house this morning." Conley slid the box across the chief's desk. "Know anything about it?"

Beads of sweat shone on Logan's head as he opened the box. His lips disappeared into a thin line. "The dead girl was missing a finger."

"Very astute of you." Conley reached across the desk and retrieved the box.

"We need that for evidence, Hook." Logan grabbed for the box.

Jo watched the two men in puzzlement. Conley stashed the box in his jacket. Logan's face flared red.

"I'll have you arrested for obstruction of justice." The big man rose to his feet. "I've read your rap sheet."

Conley copied him, leaned close and planted his hands on the desktop. "You do, and I'll blow your little operation out of the water. I know darn well you haven't done a thing to resolve that girl's murder. If I checked this precinct's unsolved missing children cases, how many would I find from here and surrounding towns?"

"How dare you," Logan sputtered.

"Conley?" Jo's gaze whipped from one man to

the other.

Lowering his voice, Conley continued. "Either you're involved in what's going on in this town, or you're being paid to keep a lid on it. I intend to prove it." He straightened. "Let's go, Jo."

Logan stepped around his desk. His speed was surprising for a man of his size. One beefy paw clamped Conley's arm. "Just one minute."

To Jo's horror, several officers on the other side of the glass rose from their desks and stepped toward them. Oh, Lord, they were going to attack. "Conley."

"Take your hand off me, Logan." He set his jaw firmly. A muscle on the left side twitched. Jo focused on this symbol of Conley's anger. It seemed to beat with the same rhythm of her quickening heart.

"I'm placing you under arrest." The man grabbed at Conley's pocket with his free hand.

"Try it and every newspaper for miles around will know about your little game." Conley shook himself free and straightened his jacket. "Jo?" His blue eyes bore into hers.

She nodded and followed him. She had to skip to keep up with his fast pace. Meredith's head turned to follow them. Her mouth hung open. Jo shrugged her shoulders and scurried out the front door after Conley.

Once they were back in the car, she asked, "What's going on? What makes you think Logan knows anything about this?"

Conley laughed. "I didn't know anything until now. I played on a hunch."

"They aren't going to look for who killed her, are they?" She looked at her folded hands lying in her lap. With Conley's next words, her heart stilled.

"They already know."

15

They passed Blake's house. Firemen sprinted toward the building. The strident ringing of fire truck alarms bounced off Jo's eardrums. The flashing of red lights cast a glow on the crowd of onlookers. Black smoke billowed above the mansion's red-tiled roof, turning the blue sky an ashy gray.

Conley stopped on the side of the road.

"Alex!" Jo fought with the door lock before yanking on the door handle and shoving the door open.

The top floor of the mansion blazed with scarlet and orange flames. Black smoke billowed from the shattered windows. Firefighters labored under yellow jackets and heavy hose.

Getting the door open, Jo leaped from the car and sprinted across the lawn, dodging firemen and sightseers. Her breath labored in her chest. Her attention remained focused on the beacon which was her son. Someone grabbed her arm, halting her and she jerked free, shoving aside an elderly lady who paused in front of her.

"Jo." Hands clutched at her again, tighter. "Jo." Conley spun her to face him. "He's there. Alex is with Blake."

She took a deep shuddering breath and turned. Blake smiled at her and lifted her son into the arms of another man who quickly deposited the boy in the backseat of a car. Alex cried out, reaching for her, and Blake slammed the door closed.

"Alex." The words burst from her in a wail, tearing at her throat.

"It's for his own safety, Jocelyn." Blake stalked across the lawn, brushing soot from his jacket. "I'm sure you don't want him around all this commotion. What if he were to be trampled?"

"I want to speak with him." She took a step toward the parked car.

"Jo, wait." Conley placed a hand on her shoulder.

With a mighty groan, the mansion's roof collapsed, shooting sparks, flames, and smoke higher into the air and over the heads of the spectators, casting the bright autumn day into cloudiness.

Jo screamed and ducked. She folded her arms over her head. Scarlet embers rained upon her, and she shrieked when one landed, burning her arm. Conley arched his body protectively over hers and drew her close to his chest.

Pandemonium reigned as firemen rushed closer to aim thick streams of water at the fire. Policemen ushered spectators further away, yelling and pushing them to the other side of the street. A child's cries rent the air.

Jo peered from under the cover of Conley's arms. Blake stood rigid, a thin smile marring his otherwise stony features. His eyes shone, reflecting the flames, and Jo shivered.

An explosion rocked the afternoon and she screamed again, burying her face in Conley's shirt. Debris rained down, thudding against the car which held Alex. With a squeal of the tires, the car backed from the drive and roared away.

Blake uttered a short grunt and plucked a shard of glass from his thigh. He frowned, staring down at the blood staining the silk fabric of his suit. With a curse, he tossed the glass to the ground and spun, limping to the paramedics.

"He's a mad man," Jo whispered, her voice hoarse with horror. She straightened, her eyes locking with Conley's. "He's crazy."

Conley nodded. "And all the more dangerous because of it."

"He was smiling as he watched the house burn." She shook her head. "Like he enjoyed it." A sourness seared her stomach. She looked down the street in the direction Alex had gone. "Alex could have been in the house."

"He wasn't." Conley handed her the inhaler

from his pocket before marching to the burning embers. A fireman reached out to stop him and Conley said a few words Jo couldn't hear. The fireman stepped back.

With the house fallen to rubbish, and the majority of the flames extinguished, the spectators soon grew bored and drifted away in small groups and low murmurs. Blake argued with the paramedic who wanted to cut away the leg of his trousers. Shaking his head, the man stepped back and waited for Blake to roll up the pant leg.

Blake cursed and fell back onto the stretcher when the fabric wouldn't roll past his knee. The paramedic sliced scissors quickly through the fabric and tossed the remnant on the ground. Blake's eyes locked with Jo's.

He smiled; a thin, cold smile that robbed Jo's bones of what autumn warmth the day provided. She folded her arms tightly around her middle.

"Let's get you out of here." Conley stepped beside her, tucking her hair behind an ear, out of her face.

She nodded, numb, and allowed him to lead her back to the Mercedes. She glanced back once more as she bent to get in the front seat. Blake still smiled at her as he sat, one bare leg wrapped in gauze. A small red stain spread across the white fibers.

*

Conley spread the comforter over a sleeping Jo's shoulders. He cupped one silken cheek in the palm of his hand and closed his eyes—just for a moment he pretended she loved him. That they had a regular marriage built on mutual love and respect. Bending, he placed a kiss on her forehead, then turned and left the room, locking the door behind him.

The rest of the house was quiet, its residents deep in slumber. The sole of his gym shoes thudded dully against the carpeted stairs. When he paused at the bottom, he could hear the soft whir of the heater as it spread warmth through the house. A night light on the wall stretched his shadow ahead of him.

Conley eased open the kitchen door leading to the garage and tensed as it creaked slightly. He paused and listened for someone to call out. He rubbed his hand along the rough surface of the wall for the light, located the switch and flicked it, illuminating the garage with a flash of light.

He searched the walls, astounded at the barrenness of the place. No lawn tools hung from the painted plaster. No paint cans stood stacked in a corner. Complete opposite of the garages he was accustomed to.

On the far wall was another door, and he stepped eagerly toward it. He tested the handle. It was unlocked. He pushed it open and grinned. Propped in one corner was a shovel, which he took. He scanned the metal shelves. His gaze lit on a group of flashlights. After grabbing the nearest one, he pulled the door closed.

Opting to walk rather than risk the sound of the car's engine waking anyone, he headed out a back door and cut across the lawn. Halfway across the manicured grounds the sprinklers came on, soaking his shoes. He groaned and sprinted into the trees that bordered the property.

Thick foliage blocked the moon, and he risked turning on the flashlight. Dogs barked as he raced behind properties. Lights flicked on. Voices called for dogs to be quiet. Conley squatted behind a bush and shivered in the evening's chill. Once the night was again dark and quiet, he rose to his feet and set off.

He breathed a prayer of thanks when he reached Blake's property and discovered it vacant. The burned house loomed before him like a mountain of freshly uncovered dinosaur bones. The acrid smell of smoke hung thick over the area and stung his nostrils.

He kicked at the fallen timbers and moved the flashlight beam from side to side. There! The tell-tale puddle shaped stain of an accelerant. Conley raised the flashlight, illuminating the taller pillars. Large, high-relief blisters covered several of the wooden beams, giving them an alligator skin appearance. The fire had been deliberately set, just as Conley suspected. But by whom? Was it Blake or someone else?

Using the shovel, Conley pushed aside several of the smaller, still smoking beams. He did this sporadically across the foundation, searching the concrete slab. After an hour, he quit and leaned against one of the few remaining pillars. His shirt stuck to his skin with sweat and his breathing was heavy. If Blake had a hiding place for abducted children, it wasn't below this house.

"Hey, you!" A floodlight brightened the area,

blinding him, and Conley threw up an arm to shade his face.

"What are you doing there?" A large, portly man climbed down from the driver's seat of a utility van. He brandished a tire iron in one hand.

Conley clicked off his own flashlight and swung the shovel to his shoulder. With a leap, he cleared the foundation and sprinted back into the trees.

*

A hand caressed her cheek, waking her. Jo smiled and stretched. "Conley." She placed her hand over his.

He sighed and grasped her hand, squeezing and grinding the fine bones together until she squeaked.

Jo reached up and turned on the light. Blake sat on the edge of the bed. No light shone in his eyes. They were as cold and hard as the sapphire ring he'd once given her. One final, painful squeeze and he released her.

"Where's Conley?" Jo drew the blankets up under her chin.

"Don't hide, dear. I've seen it all before." He whipped the covers from her. "I have no idea where your dear Conley is. I had intended to surprise you both, but, alas, you're alone."

"Where's Alex?" Jo scanned the room. She searched for a weapon of some kind.

"Safe." He trailed a finger down the satin covering her leg. He sighed again and rose to pace the room. He fingered the few items on her dresser as he muttered to himself. She strained to make out his words and willed her heart to quiet.

"All I want is for her to love me. Why can't she? If she loved me, I wouldn't have to do this." He whirled to face her. "Do you realize that? If you loved me, you could prevent all this."

"Prevent what?" Despite her efforts not to, her voice trembled.

"This!" he roared and whipped his arm across the top of the dresser, scattering her toiletries.

Jo sat up and scooted back against the headboard. She drew her knees to her chest and wrapped her arms around them.

Blake continued to pace, alternating between yells and mutters. Jo's heart pounded hard enough to rock her body, sending her back and forth on waves of apprehension. A sob caught in her throat, and she choked it back.

Whirling to face her, Blake jumped to the bed beside her. Grabbing a fistful of her hair, he yanked her face close to his. "Are you crying? Good. I want you to shed tears for me."

"You're hurting me." Tears sprang to her eyes as he tugged again. He'd eaten a mint recently. Its peppermint smell drifted across her face as he breathed.

"As you've hurt me?" He released his hold on her hair and shoved her away from him. Her skull hit the headboard with a resounding thud.

Jo lifted a shaking hand to the back of her head. "Where's my son?" she asked softly.

"You sound like a broken record. Where's Alex? Where's Alex?" Blake laughed, braying. The sound rang inside Jo's aching head. "He's not here. I've already answered that question." His voice rose. "Stop asking it."

"Why am I so important to you? There are plenty of women who would be willing to be your wife." She reached for the blankets. His eyes narrowed when she did, and she rewrapped her arms around her knees, trying to still her shivering.

The blow to the side of her head knocked her sideways. Her teeth clicked together, and she bit her tongue. She rolled, stopping only when she hit the floor. Her breath left her lungs in a whoosh, and the metallic taste of blood filled her mouth. Her tongue throbbed and she struggled to breathe.

"I want you! You. You're mine! I *chose* you." Blake grabbed her by the upper arm. His fingers dug into the tender flesh, and he yanked her to her feet. "Once your *precious* Conley is out of the picture, you'll realize you belong to me."

Her eyes focused on the drop of spittle dangling from his bottom lip. It quavered as he spoke. She swallowed the bile of her fear as her heart cried out for Conley.

Blake lowered his head. His mouth crushed hers. His teeth ground against her lips, adding more pain to her mouth. Jo went limp. Visions flashed through her mind. Other men, some young, some old, spun like the reel of an old movie. Blake was there, as a young man, before their marriage. His image swam and was lost among the endless faces of the others.

With a shriek, she planted the palms of her hands on his chest and shoved him back. "You were there. I remember." She wiped his kiss viciously from her lips. "You *did* choose me. I was lined up like a doll on display, and you bought me." She grabbed the lamp from beside the bed and hurled it at his head.

He ducked and dove for her and taking her to the floor. "You should feel honored." He grabbed at her gown, ripping the delicate fabric.

Kicking and screaming, she doubled her fist and swung, connecting with his chin. The impact sent shock waves up her arm. He swore and took control of her flailing hands, pinning them above her head.

"Let...go...of...me. You will not use me again. Ever." The fury of her struggle left her breathless. Her chest heaved. "I will not let fear rule me ever again. And if you hurt my son, I will kill you."

Blake lowered his face to hers again. She sunk her teeth into his bottom lip.

He roared and leaned back, raising his fist. His handsome features twisted, and his eyes shone with a murderous light as he whispered, "If I can't have you, neither will he."

"Get off her." Conley tossed the smaller man across the room. Blake crashed into the wall. He spared a quick glance at Jo before lifting the fallen man by the shirt front.

Conley's face reddened. His jaws clenched. Rearing

171

back, he slammed Blake to the wall again.

Blake's head dented the plaster, raining flecks of white onto his dark head. He laughed. "I came for you big guy. I came to kill you."

"What's stopping you?" Conley released him. "I'm here." He stepped back. His muscles flexed and quivered beneath his tee shirt.

His head snapped back with the first of Blake's punches. Blood smeared across his lip, and he grinned. "That all you got? You didn't even knock me off my feet."

Blake roared and charged.

Conley's leg shot out, tripping him and landing him on his back. As Blake lay there, Conley stepped over him. He planted a booted foot on the man's wounded thigh. "How does it feel having someone bigger than you pin you to the ground like a bug? I'd like to squash you." He increased pressure and Blake gasped.

"No, Conley." Jo wrapped a blanket around her shoulders and stood beside him. "He isn't worth it. You know how the people in this town are. He'll twist the story, and you'll go to jail. Prestige loves Blake. His family used to own the land this town sits on."

For a moment, Conley stared at her then lifted his foot. Blake scurried to his feet.

"She's used goods." He set his chin, lifting it slightly to look into Conley's face. "Trained in *every* way to please me. To know what *I* want." He jumped back as Conley jerked toward him. "Let me know how you enjoy my cast off." Blake straightened his shirt and smoothed his mussed hair. He cast a thin smile at Jo, and left.

Her legs shook and gave way beneath her. Jo collapsed on the edge of the bed. "He bought me, Conley." She stared at her bare feet. "Like a piece of property he went out and purchased. I remember. I wasn't alone. There were others. Boys and girls. I was young. Maybe eight or ten. Maybe even younger. My parents were there, only they weren't my parents then…I don't think. I don't know." She raised a tear-stained face to his. "Blake pointed at me and said 'I want this one.' Who am I, Conley?"

He sat next to her and gathered her in his arms. "I don't know. But there's a lot going on here, Jo. The pieces are beginning to fall together, but they're still pieces."

"Where were you?" she sniffed.

"Collecting some of those pieces." He rubbed her back. "The fire at Blake's was deliberately set. I found traces of accelerant."

"Why would Blake burn down his own house?"

"I don't know that he did. Maybe he's covering up. Maybe he's made someone mad at him."

Jo shivered. "Where are my…Harold and Sylvia?" She couldn't think of them as her parents anymore.

Conley shrugged. "I haven't seen them." He placed his fingers under her chin and tilted her face to his. "Are you all right?"

She nodded. "I want to leave here. We'll stay in a hotel until we get Alex back."

"Good idea." He rose from the bed and held out his

hand. "But once your parents show up, I've got a few questions for Sylvia Woodward."

"Why her?" Jo stepped into the closet to change and gather their things.

"Harold's tougher."

"Really?" She pocked her head around the corner. "He's always seemed like such a pushover."

"Tough as nails."

Jo withdrew into the closet and leaned against the wall. It was difficult to picture Harold as tough. Throughout her childhood, Sylvia seemed to run the house. Was Jo missing something? She wracked her brain, sorting through facts and memories, trying to dig up something to support Conley's statement. Her head ached from the banging against the headboard. Her thoughts made no sense.

The knowledge of the two people she'd grown up thinking were her parents, and now knowing they weren't, at least biologically, sent her heart plummeting. With a heavy sigh she dropped the ripped gown on the floor and wondered for the thousandth time where God was.

16

Jo dropped her suitcase on yet another hotel bed and flopped down beside it.

"This isn't having the effect I thought it would."

"What?" Conley placed his own suitcase in the closet.

"I thought Blake would give me back my son if he knew I was married."

Conley turned and stared at her. "You actually thought it would be that easy?"

She sat up. "It was your idea."

"I said that our being married would make it harder for him to claim custody. I suspected something wasn't right when your parents hired me. Sure, Blake legally adopted Alex, but if you had a man in the picture, maybe there would be somebody out there who might listen and start to ask questions." He stood in front of her. "We can go get Alex right now. We'll go to another city. Get the police there to help us and walk away from what we know is going on in this town."

Jo peered at him beneath lowered lashes. "I just want my son."

"Then let's go get him. Do you have any idea where he is now?"

"No." She bit her lip to prevent the words from bursting forth, but spill out they did. "You're using my son as bait. You asked me to marry you, then brought me here to use Alex to glorify your career." She stood, hands propped on her hips, and faced him. "Well, it won't work. You can leave. I don't even know who you are."

Conley looked down at her, stunned. His face changed from one of disbelief, to surprise, then reddened with anger. His eyes narrowed and a muscle twitched in his jaw. "I'll leave when I'm good and ready." He put a hand on her shoulder and forced her back to a sitting position on the bed. "You're right. I can't walk away from what is going on here, but I would never jeopardize Alex. I know in my gut that Blake won't hurt him. If you can look me in the eye and tell me that our being together hasn't helped you...then, fine, I'll leave."

Her lips tightened, and Jo's eyes clashed with Conley's. "You know I can't say that."

He bent, his face inches from hers. "And if you can say that our coming back here and stirring things up hasn't been beneficial in you remembering things..."

"I never knew I forgot them." She stood,

maintaining eye contact.

"Well, now you do."

"You have a temper problem. I've been watching whenever you get angry. Your body gets all tense, your face gets red…"

Conley clamped his mouth closed. A slow smile spread across his face, and Jo's heart did a flip-flop in her chest. "I think we're having our first marital fight."

She licked dry lips. "We are?"

He nodded and took a step closer. "Definitely. Want to make up?" He reached for her and pulled her close. Conley lowered his head. Jo focused on her growing reflection in his pupils. When his lips claimed hers, she shut her eyes.

This wasn't a mere brush of lips across lips or a chaste kiss on the cheek. He flattened her against him, bending her slightly at the waist and sending her emotions reeling. She gasped when he released her mouth and transferred his lips to her ear lobe then trailed down her neck.

"Not fair," she whispered.

He laughed, low and deep. His lips traveled back to her mouth, now not demanding, but slow and thoughtful. Her legs weakened, and she sagged against him, shocked at the way her body awakened to his kiss. Her heart thudded in her throat, and her world spun.

"Stop," she gasped. "I can't breathe."

"Good." He increased the intensity of his kisses and lowered her to the bed. "Do you want me to stop?" he whispered, lifting his head. His breath blew against her tingling lips.

Mutely, she shook her head.

Conley slid his hand behind her, entangling it in her hair. His gaze locked on hers, then lowered again.

*

She woke hours later, the sun setting in the sky, and stretched. Jo turned her head. Conley lay next to her, his gaze on her. "Were you watching me sleep?"

"Yes. You're beautiful."

She lifted a hand to her hair and tried to pat it into place. "I'm sleep mussed."

Leaning forward, he kissed her. Butterflies danced in her stomach. "I never knew it could be like that."

"I'd like to make you aware of a lot more, Jo."

She snuggled closer. Her head fit in the curve of his shoulder. "There's no going back for me. Not now."

"I don't want to." With his finger, he tilted her face to his. "I never had any intention of going back. This is what I want, Jo. *You* are what I want. I love you. I have from the first moment I laid eyes on you."

She warmed at his words, but didn't reciprocate. What a foreign concept. Somebody wanting her—for her. But did she love him? He gave her a feeling of security, of safety, but was that all? He aroused feelings in her she'd never experienced before. These things in her marriage to Blake had been rough. Her feelings had never entered into the act. The faces of all the unknown men whirled through her brain and she shivered, squirming closer. "How did you get to be so kind?"

"I'm not kind, just truthful. You were right when

you said I have an anger problem. I spent a lot of time in solitary confinement working it out. That's where I met God. I prayed for Him to help me control it." He rolled over to his back, keeping one arm around her and folding one behind his head. "Took God a while to get my attention."

Jo sighed. "God doesn't pay much attention to me, I'm afraid. Life keeps dealing me trial after trial."

"He sent me, didn't He?" Conley gave her a squeeze.

She tilted her head and peered at him. "Yes, He did." Her throat convulsed. Tears threatened to spill. "Everything's going to be okay, isn't it?"

"I think so. But, Jo, Alex isn't the only one we need to focus on here. We need to stop this thing. You know that, don't you?"

She twirled one finger in the light colored hairs on his chest. "I know." His stomach rumbled, and she giggled. "Hungry?"

"For you. Food can wait." He pulled her on top of him and drew her face close to his.

Jo woke the next morning, still wrapped in the new-found warmth of Conley's love. She smiled and stretched, lifting her arms above her head before opening her eyes. Her hand brushed against an empty pillow. She started upright, then heard the reassuring sound of the shower and allowed herself to fall back onto the pillows.

He'd told her he loved her. Was she capable of loving a man? She had no doubt of her feelings of safety with Conley. The emotions that swept over her during their lovemaking, she couldn't begin to describe. But, love? She didn't think she was capable. Would Conley be satisfied with anything less than her total love for him?

She rolled onto her side and clutched his pillow to her chest. During her marriage to Blake, she'd allowed him his husbandly "rights", having been drilled by her mother on the proper acts of a good wife. Her lips twisted. She'd been well experienced by then. She closed her eyes, the past horror washing over her. Bile, hot and sour threatened to rise.

"Good morning." Conley placed a tender kiss on her lips.

She opened her eyes and smiled at the warm look in his eyes. Her discomfort instantly receded. "Good morning."

"Ready for breakfast? I ordered room service."

"Wonderful. I'm starved." Jo sat up and snatched at the sheet on the bed. She stopped at the sight of the white linen robe draped across the back of a nearby chair. Conley always thought of everything.

He held the robe while she slid her arms into it, and Jo turned toward the small round dining table. A distraught woman on the television caught her attention and she turned the volume louder. "Conley, look at this." Behind the woman, off to the side, were the burned remains of Blake's house.

Conley placed an arm around Jo's shoulders and she pressed closer to him as they listened to the crying woman plead for the return of her children. Her heart sank to the pit of her stomach. "It's Blake's neighbor. They've taken her children." She craned her neck to look into her husband's face. "We've got to do something."

"It's time to put some pressure on your mother. She knows something. I'm convinced of it, and I think she's scared."

Reaching for a hot roll from a covered basket, Jo shook her head. "Sylvia Woodward isn't afraid of anything."

"I think she is. The toughness is just a cover." Conley stretched across the table and poured her a cup of fragrant coffee, strong with the scent of Hazelnut.

She spread butter on one half of a hot roll. It melted into the soft valleys. "Okay. I'll put the pressure on her after breakfast."

"Do you want me to go with you? I don't like the idea of you going anywhere alone."

"I need to do this. I need to put to rest some very active ghosts."

"I'll drive you and wait outside."

She opened her mouth to protest and clamped it shut at the warning look in his eyes. "Fine."

Jo laughed, the sound shrill and nervous. She glanced at her parents' house, then up at Conley. "I'm nervous."

He squeezed her arm. "I can still go with you."

"No. I need to do this. Her guard will be down if I

go alone."

Conley lowered his head and kissed her. "I'm right out here if you need me."

She reached up and cupped her palm around his cheek. "Thank you."

The walk to the front door seemed never ending, and Jo's heart rate seemed to accelerate with each step. Her pulse pounded in her ears. The massive oak door towered over her, and she hesitated before reaching for the door knob. She jumped back as the door swung open.

"Good afternoon, Jocelyn."

"Sylvia."

Sylvia's eyes hardened, resembling blue ice. "Don't be ridiculous. I'm still your mother." She held the door open wider. "Come in. We'll sit in the living room."

With trembling legs, Jo followed her mother. A tea tray with a pot and cups sat on the coffee table next to a tray of tiny sandwiches. "Are you expecting company?"

"I was. Tea?"

"Please." Jo sat on the edge of the sofa. Her mother quietly handed her a tea cup and saucer, then held out the tray of sandwiches.

"I'm assuming, since you left so abruptly last night, that something is on your mind and you are determined to speak to me about it."

Jo's cup clattered against the saucer as she set it down. "Some children disappeared."

"I heard it on the news." Sylvia lifted her cup to her

lips. "Tragic."

"You aren't going to make this easy, are you?"

Finely arched brows rose over Sylvia's eyes.

"I want to know how you got me. I want to know how you could sit back and let me be used the way I was. I want to know how you could sit there and be silent when Blake beat me."

"Jocelyn." Sylvia set her cup down and folded her hands in her lap. "Children are adopted every day and their true parentage not revealed. What is so wrong about my wanting a child? I'm sorry if I should have told you we weren't your biological parents, but—a"

"It's the abuse that's so wrong." Adopted or not, Jocelyn should have grown up in a loving home.

"We never abused you. We gave you everything a child could want. The best of everything. We *saved* you from a life of abuse, if anything. As for your marriage, it wasn't our place to step in and interfere…"

"Interfere?" Jo stood and paced the room.

"Women would die to be in your shoes."

She whirled to face her mother. "And probably were dying. This is ridiculous." Jo flung her arms in the air and stepped forward. She stopped inches from her mother's crossed legs. She bent and brought her face close to the other woman's. "Would you like to know who Alex's father is?"

Sylvia's composure slipped, and she shook her head.

"Your brother. Uncle Dave is Alex's father. Maybe you did 'rescue' me from a life of child prostitution, but you put me right smack into incest!" Jo straightened and turned away. "You turned a blind eye to it, just as you're turning a blind eye to it now." She spun to meet Sylvia's stunned eyes. "Where are the missing children?"

"I...I don't know." Sylvia dropped her eyes to her lap.

"If you don't answer my question, I'll have Conley beat it out of you."

Sylvia's head snapped up. "Jocelyn!"

"Well." She crossed her arms.

"I don't know where those children are. I didn't know about my brother. I can't believe you would even think that I could condone that type of behavior with my daughter." Sylvia took a deep breath. "I did know what we took you from, but to my knowledge, Blake isn't, wasn't, involved." She stiffened her neck. "I had no idea of the things you were going through. You were always a silent, withdrawn—"

"I don't believe you."

Sylvia shrugged and looked away. "I can not help that."

"How old was I?" A sob caught in Jo's throat. "How old was I when you took me from that life?"

"Eight."

Jo's knees gave way and she fell back to the sofa. "Who are my parents?"

"I have no idea." Sylvia took a deep breath. "I wanted a child so badly, and I couldn't have one. Harold brought me you. He said he saved you." She lifted eyes that shimmered with unshed tears. "You were beautiful. All those crazy curls and those big brown eyes." She shrugged and turned away. "We gave you a privileged life, Jocelyn. You have no reason to complain."

Jo stared at her mother in stunned disbelief. "No reason to…" She rose woodenly from the sofa and forced words from her throat. "You've done this my whole life. For as long as I can remember you've turned a blind eye to what went on around you. You're content to sit safely wrapped in your warm cocoon of wealth. Well, *Mother*, I'm done. Finished. Thank you for the 'privileged' life you've given me. The trust fund will come in handy. But best of all." Jo smiled. "Thank you for hiring that wonderful man waiting outside to fetch me back. I will find my son, and when I do, I'll leave this place and never return."

She turned and opened the front door to dash down the sidewalk and into Conley's arms. Sobs wracked her body, and he reached around her to open the car door.

Putting his hand on her head, Conley helped her into the backseat then scooted in beside her. He pulled her into his lap and wrapped his arms tight around her. "Shhh."

She sniffed. "She says she doesn't know where the children are. She's oblivious, Conley. It was a total waste of time."

"You did great. It wasn't a waste of time. Sylvia knows more than she's letting on."

Jo raised her head from his chest. "I told her

who Alex's father is. Considering it's her brother, she was pretty unresponsive."

A sharp rap on the window startled Jo, and she whirled. Her head collided with Conley's.

Holding a hand to his head, Conley pushed the button and lowered the window.

"How quaint," Blake sneered. "Making out in the parent's front yard." He glanced around them. "And in broad daylight."

"Well, you know newlyweds." Conley withdrew his hand from his head, glanced at it, then turned back to Blake. "Can we help you?"

"I'm just returning home." Blake tossed his head. "I'm staying here now that my house burned. Hotel don't do much for me."

"Where's Alex?" Jo's head jerked in his direction.

"Safe." Blake waved his hand. "Why are you always so concerned? If I intended to harm the boy, I would have left him in the house to burn."

Jo slid from Conley's lap. "You and Sylvia enjoy the tea."

"Tea?"

Conley swung the car door open. Blake jumped back. "We were just leaving, Nielson. Have a good day." He swung his long legs from the car and unfolded to stand before the shorter man. His shoulder clipped Blake as he reached to open the driver's door. "Excuse me."

Blake's eyes narrowed, then turned to Jo. She started to crawl from the back seat, thought better of it, and climbed over into the front passenger side. She risked another glance over her shoulder. Blake had taken another step back, his gaze still frozen on her. She shivered, and faced out the front window.

*

Blake closed the door softly behind him. Sylvia sat hunched over on the sofa, her hands folded in her lap.

"Hello, Dave." Her voice barely carried across the room.

"It's not Dave." Blake strode across the room and sat in the chair across from her. He leaned back and crossed one leg over the other. He eyed the tea set on the table. "Pour me a cup."

Taking a deep, shaky breath, Sylvia lifted her head and reached for the teapot.

"What did you tell her, Sylvia?"

"Nothing." Her hand shook as she poured tea into a porcelain cup. "I played dumb, as usual." Her eyes flicked to a spot over Blake's shoulder.

A chill ran up his spine and his hand froze, suspended toward the cup Sylvia now offered him. Slowly he turned his head. "Dave."

A large man with balding head and black glasses stood just where Blake couldn't see him as he entered the room. A breeze blew through the French doors the man had entered by, ruffling the curtains. The smile on Dave's face chilled his heart.

"Boss is mad at you, Blake." Dave took the cup from Blake's hand. "Your obsession with your ex-wife has your brain scrambled."

Blake fought to hold his features in check. A sign of weakness would be like a match to gasoline where Dave was concerned. "I have two children in hold right now."

"From our own town." Dave poured the tea into his mouth. "You're slipping. That's against the rules, and you know it." He clattered the cup onto the tray. "Don't make us resort to drastic measures." He cupped Sylvia's cheek with one meaty paw and kissed her. "I've missed you, dear sister. Heard our little darling is back, and can't wait to reacquaint myself with her." He smacked Sylvia's cheek, leaving a pink imprint of his hand. "I'll be back for dinner."

Blake released the breath he wasn't aware he'd been holding. His legs cramped from being crossed, and he painfully straightened them. A sob escaped Sylvia, and she buried her face in her hands.

Rolling his eyes, Blake stood. Stupid woman stayed. She was obviously content with her life, so why the pretense of grief? "I'm going out." He slammed the door behind him and marched around the corner to where he'd parked his car.

Anger replaced fear as he drove. This time out of Prestige. Headlights from oncoming traffic blinked through slots in the interstate median.

Stupid woman! Without his protection as her husband, she'll be back in Dave's hands. He pounded the steering wheel and pressed harder on the accelerator. The boss's right hand man will kill Hook and take Jo right back into what Blake had saved her from.

Red neon lights flashed a truck stop, and he pulled

his Volvo around to the back of the restaurant. The night grew late and patrons were few. A side door provided him entry next to the restrooms, and he stood in the shadows with his hands thrust into his pockets.

People came and went. Mothers bringing their daughters. Fathers bringing their sons. A clock chimed eleven before opportunity knocked.

She looked to be around twelve with straight red hair smoothed back from her face with a yellow headband. She spotted Blake. Her eyes flickered from him to the restroom door.

17

Jo rolled over, laying her arm across Conley's waist and her ear against his chest. She listened to the thud of his heartbeat. Felt the gentle rise and fall of his chest. How could she have fallen so quickly for a man she knew so little about? How was it possible for her to be so free with him considering the atrocities of her past? What had he done to begin the healing of her heart?

Conley had mentioned he believed Blake's house fire had been deliberate. Why? Jo wracked her brain, digging for information from her past. What kind of game was her ex-husband playing? The role of martyr or rescuer? She sighed and rolled over to her back. Sleep, clouded in confusion, finally claimed her.

The bugs were back. Their whispers drowned out all other sound. Jo's breath rattled in her chest as she slapped the insects from her face and hair. Where was she? She needed to focus. Her eyes strained to peer through the engulfing darkness. Louder scurries to her left caused her to whip in the direction of the sound. Whimpers rose in the darkness.

She wasn't alone. There were others with her. Other children huddled in the darkness with the insects. She rose to her feet and kept one hand on the crawling, dirt wall beside her. She called out. Others answered, and she crunched her way, using the wall to guide her. Something landed on her head. She screamed.

"Jo." She slapped at the hands grasping her shoulders.

"Jo. It's me."

She opened her eyes. Conley leaned over her. Her gaze locked with his and her breathing slowed, regulating. "The dream. I wasn't alone. There were others there with me, but I couldn't reach them."

"Shhh." He pulled her into his arms, smoothing her hair. "It's all right. I'm here. There's no one else."

"But there was." Jo pulled back. She searched his face. "It's not just a dream, Conley. I think it's a memory. I was put into a hole when I was a child. There were other children with me. I'm certain of it. The dark was so complete I couldn't see anything. I could only feel the insects. Why? Why would they throw us into a hole?"

"To subdue you? To frighten you?"

"I remember being blinded by light when they came to get me. I can't remember where they took me. I know I wasn't put back in there, though." She placed her head in her hands. "It doesn't make sense. I need to remember."

"You will. Being back in Prestige will force the memories." Conley slid his legs over the side of the bed. "I just pray you can handle them when they come."

"I have to." A horrifying thought grabbed her in its icy clutches. She held the sheet close to her chest. "You don't think Blake will put Alex in that hole, do you?"

"We'll pray he doesn't. I think that's only where they put their new acquisitions." He placed a calming hand on her shoulder. "You'll feel better after some breakfast."

Jo nodded and rolled from the bed. "Who do you think phoned me five years ago? The person who warned me about Blake? That's why I left, did I tell you? A call came warning me that Blake was involved in something dangerous. Evil. Something that involved missing children."

"I think it was Sylvia."

"My mother?" Jo shook her head. "Impossible. She's always sided with Blake. Hasn't gotten over the fact I left him. It's all about appearances with my mother."

"Maybe it's an act. Something tells me Sylvia is afraid. Very afraid."

Jo paused to remember the voice on the phone. Low and whispered. "It could have been her, I guess. I'd like to think there's some good in Sylvia Woodward. Now, my father, him I can't figure out." She reached for a lightweight sweater dress. "I felt loved by her as a child. It's her behavior now that confuses me." And the way her mother changed the moment her father, Uncle Dave, or Blake stepped into the room. Then, Sylvia's nurturing ended.

Conley slipped a shirt over his head. "I think Sylvia is as much a victim as you are. She protected you the best she could."

"Maybe." Jo stepped to the bathroom vanity and picked up a hairbrush. She ran it through her curls. "You're starting to convince me." Who were her biological parents? How long had they searched for her? Why hadn't she been found? Especially once she started school. Somebody, somewhere, should have recognized her and called out an alarm.

"Here let me." Conley took the brush from her hand, sliding it through her hair with long steady strokes.

"Mmmm." Jo closed her eyes. "That feels really good."

"You have a lot of electricity in your hair. It crackles like fire."

Jo met his gaze through the mirror. "When I was young, I'd brush it in the dark so I could see the sparks. I didn't feel so alone then." Tutors. She'd had private tutors. No childhood friends other than close friends of the family. That's how she'd been kept a secret.

"You're not alone now." He set the brush on the counter and wrapped his arms around her. His chin rested on top of her head. "Ready?"

"In a minute. Let me put on my makeup."

"You don't need any makeup. You're beautiful au

naturale."

"You're biased, and I feel better with it on."

He let his arms slide away from her. "Okay. Five minutes."

"I need more time than that."

"Okay, ten. I'm starving."

*

Jo idly pushed the pancakes swimming in syrup around on her plate. Melancholy covered her like a heavy blanket she couldn't shake off. Her shoulders slumped. Pulling herself upright, she blurted, "How are you at peace all the time?"

After swallowing the food in his mouth, Conley met her gaze. "God."

"I know, but…"

"Jo." He leaned back against the red vinyl of the diner booth. "God's peace surpasses all understanding. I can't do it on my own. I've tried and failed every time."

She let her fork fall with a clatter to her plate. "That just isn't the God I grew up with. My parents taught me about a God of vengeance. One who rules with an iron fist. One who turned his back on my 'sin' of having an illegitimate child." She shook her head. "I don't understand your God of love."

"For one thing, getting pregnant wasn't your choice, and even if it were, God can easily forgive that sin. Look at King David and Bathsheba. Didn't God forgive them for adultery and murder?"

"Yes."

"Then why can't you believe He'd forgive you?

Especially since you're an innocent victim." Conley reached across the table and took both of her hands in his. "Have you asked Him?"

Tears welled in Jo's eyes. "No. I've been too ashamed. Too stubborn. Fighting to do everything on my own. This God you describe sounds too good to be true."

"He is. But that doesn't change anything. Would you like to pray?"

She blinked against the tears. "Here?"

"Why not?"

"There're people around."

"So?" Conley glanced around them. "They aren't paying any attention to us."

"Okay." A lump formed in Jo's throat, and she grabbed her glass of water to wash it down. "I'm ready."

Conley laughed. "You're not going to the guillotine, Jo." He squeezed her hands and began to pray. When he'd finished, he pulled on her hands until she leaned across the table. He bent forward and kissed her. "I love you, you know. You are something truly special. I'm grateful to your parents for hiring me." With that, he released her hands and grasped his fork. "You really are special."

The love and warmth in his eyes seared her soul, and Jo found her eyes tearing up again. She grabbed the napkin next to her plate and wiped her eyes. Why couldn't she say those three words back to him? She sighed. She loved the way her husband made her feel.

Would he still love her once Blake and his group were brought to justice? Once he'd fulfilled the task he felt he needed to accomplish? Once he'd finished saving her?

"What is it, Jo?" His blue eyes were filled with compassion.

Shrugging, she replied, "Doesn't it bother you that I can't reply back that I love you?"

"Not really. It's only a matter of time." He winked. "I'll wait. Your loving me or not doesn't change the way I feel."

Jo glanced around the diner at the people sitting at the breakfast bar, the waitresses pouring coffee, and the men and women perusing menus. How simple their lives seemed. Murmurs of conversation drifted across the room along with the clanking of silverware and squeaking of vinyl. The aroma of perking coffee and sizzling bacon wafted in the air.

The bell over the diner door tinkled and Jo turned her attention in that direction. Blake, with one hand on her son's shoulder, strolled in. His eyes immediately sought her. She was reminded of Conley's analogy of Blake having shark eyes. Void. Without emotion.

"Mommy!" Alex lurched away from Blake and propelled himself into Jo's arms.

She grabbed her son and smothered his face with kisses before pulling him closer. She wanted to draw him into herself. Back inside where she could keep him safe. The tears which had threatened all morning now ran down her face with the force of a dam unleashed. "Oh, baby."

Blake slid into the booth beside Jo and Alex. He laid his arm across the back of the seat. His fingers brushed against her shoulders, and she stiffened. Her gaze lifted to meet the hardened one of Conley.

"I suggest you move away from my wife." Conley's tone matched the coldness in his usually warm eyes.

A red flush inched its way up his neck, and Jo noticed the warning tick in his cheek. She scooted as far from Blake as she could, dragging Alex with her.

"Come on, Hook. We both know your marriage is one of name only. Jocelyn would never betray me with a man of your…stature, shall we say." Blake removed his arm and folded his hands on the table. He glanced at their breakfast plates, mouth curling with derision. "I have to admit, though, I was surprised to find Jocelyn eating in this type of establishment."

Jo's arms tightened around her son until he squirmed in protest. Her stomach churned, threatening to lose what little she'd eaten. The very air of the diner dropped several degrees when Blake entered, and she shivered.

"What kind of game are you playing?" Conley folded his arms across his chest. His biceps bulged beneath his tee shirt, hinting at the strength Jo knew he possessed.

"Game? I'm not playing any game. As I'm sure you're aware, I no longer have a home for my son to reside in." He unfolded his hands and caressed Jo's cheek. She grimaced and turned away. "My wife seems to be inclined to remain in Prestige. I felt it safe to return Alex to her."

"God's peace, God's peace," Jo muttered into her son's hair.

"What's that?" Blake's head whipped in her direction.

"Nothing." Her words barely rose above a whisper. She so desired to slide from the booth and run with Alex as far as she could, even if she had to slide under the table to do so.

"Okay, you've delivered Alex. You can go now." Conley jerked his head in the direction of the door.

"Oh, very well." Blake slid from the booth. "I happen to have a very full day ahead of me. I'll be in contact, Jocelyn. Please do us both a favor and don't skip town this time." He gave her a thin smile.

"Can we go now?" Jo stared at Blake's retreating back. "Somewhere far from Prestige?"

"I thought we talked about this." Conley shifted in his seat in order to retrieve his wallet. "I thought you wanted to help the missing children. We can't do that if your memory doesn't return, and your memory may not return if we're not in Prestige."

"I know, but I'm so afraid." Her voice cracked. "My relying on God isn't going to happen overnight."

Conley tossed money on the table and rose then extended his hand for Jo to take. "We'll be fine. So, now that there's three of us, is it back to the hotel, or to your parents?"

"Alex, where would you like to go?" Jo slid him out of the booth ahead of her. "Where do you think the three of us should live?"

The little boy thought, his right hand cupping his chin. "Can't we get our own place? That daddy is mean." He slipped his hand into Conley's large one. "I like this new one much better."

"You do, huh, Squirt?" Conley swung the boy up and onto his shoulders. "I'm kind of fond of you myself. Our own place it is. Jo, is there an apartment complex somewhere around here?"

"Not real close, but there may be a condo for rent. It'll be expensive. Everything in Prestige is." The sight of her son on Conley's shoulders lifted her feeling of oppression, and she found herself smiling.

"Money's no worry, Jo. I may be a lowly private eye, but I've got money." He placed his free hand along the small of her back. The other gripped Alex's ankles. "My parents left me a chunk when they died. I just happen to enjoy my work and saw no reason to become one of the idle rich."

"I wasn't worried about the money." Jo frowned. "My trust fund is large enough."

"Don't get prickly." He pushed the door open with his hip. "I'm just letting you know I'm not destitute."

"Well, neither am I."

"Are you guys fighting?" Alex's brow wrinkled.

"No, baby. We aren't fighting. Just disagreeing."

"Good. Cause Daddy Blake yelled a lot. It hurt my ears."

*

"Isn't there anything even moderately priced in this town?" Conley scowled after climbing into the backseat of the realtor's car. He clutched several real estate fliers in his hand.

"I believe you said money was no object, Mr. Hook." The realtor, Ms. Tavish, a plump heavily made-up woman, pursed her lips.

"I didn't mean outrageous."

"Conley." Jo turned to frown at him from the front seat.

"Prestige, as its name states, is an upstanding community," Ms. Tavish continued. She peered at Conley through the rearview mirror. "If the price is more than you can afford, perhaps we should try someplace else?"

"We want to stay in Prestige." He stared out the window as the realtor merged the luxury car with the traffic.

A dark blue, mid-size sedan pulled in behind them. Conley's eyes narrowed as he tried to discern the driver's features.

Alex bounded to his knees on the seat beside him. "What are you looking at? That car?"

"Yes, and you should be in your seat belt." Conley turned the boy around and clicked the belt around him.

"That's Daddy Blake's friend."

Conley twisted to see the car again. "Are you sure?"

"Yep. That's the man who took me away from mommy."

At her son's words, Jo whipped around. "Is he following us?"

"Pretty sure he is." Conley kept his gaze locked on the blue car.

"He isn't going to take Alex again, is he?" Jo's eyes widened.

"I don't think so. Not after Blake handed him over to us." Conley laid a hand on the boy's shoulder.

"Shall we ditch them?" Ms. Tavish tossed a glance over her shoulder.

"Excuse me?" Jo's mouth fell open.

The woman patted the Cadillac's dashboard. "This baby has a V-8 engine." The car sped forward with a roar. Jo screamed as the woman took a corner sharply. Tires squealed.

Conley smiled. "I don't think that's necessary, Ms. Tavish, but we do thank you."

She eased on the accelerator. "Are you sure? I love opening up my baby, and there are precious few opportunities to see what she can do."

"I'm sure." He gave another glance out the window. "Prestige isn't that big. They'll find us anyway. We don't want to chance getting into an accident."

"I took defensive driving lessons, Mr. Hook. That wouldn't happen." The woman's shoulders slumped in apparent defeat, and a chuckle escaped Conley. People never ceased to amaze him.

The fourth house Ms. Tavish stopped them at was a two-story Victorian cottage style with a wrap around porch and turret. Jo squealed with delight and flung the car door open. Conley followed suit, his hand wrapped around Alex's. He knew without Jo speaking a word that this would be their house.

The realtor opened the door to the sunshine yellow house and ushered them inside to welcoming oak floors and faded rose wallpaper. She turned with a smug smile. "This is one of the cheaper homes on the market."

"We'll take it." Jo clapped her hands together.

"Don't you want to have a look around?" The realtor's heels clicked on the polished wood as she led them through the downstairs, pointing out rooms. Alex wasted no time in running ahead. "There are three bedrooms and two and a half baths. The house has a parlor and large kitchen. It is approximately three thousand square feet, not counting the unfinished attic or basement. The lot is large, with a pond and trees out back."

"We'll take it," Jo stated again.

"Fine. I have the paperwork here. Anything I forgot, you can take care of later. You did say you were paying cash, correct?"

"Yes, ma'am." Conley stepped forward and put an arm across Jo's shoulders.

"Wonderful." She directed them where to sign and waited while Jo wrote a check. Ms. Tavish handed Conley the keys. "Mr. Nielson will be very pleased to have this house off the market."

"Mr. Nielson?" Conley's heart dropped to his stomach as he clutched the keys. The metal dug into his palm.

"Why, yes. Mr. Nielson listed this house last year. Such a shame for this little darling to remain vacant, but so many folks around here want something larger. They just don't want to invest the time in redoing the attic or basement." The woman glanced from Conley to Jo. "I assumed with your wife having once been married to Mr. Nielson, she would have known."

Jo shook her head. "I had no idea." The three of them turned as the doorbell rang.

"Do you want to back out?" Conley searched her face.

She smiled. "No. I have no memories of this place. It doesn't matter who once owned it. Blake or my parents probably own over half this town." She extended her hand to the realtor. "Thank you. I'm sure we'll be very happy here."

18

Jo and Conley attempted to settle into a routine of family life. She stayed home, schooled Alex, because she was afraid to let him out of her sight, and Conley disappeared for hours in his unstoppable quest to locate what he believed to be Blake's holding tank for kidnapped children. Not an easy task with most of the town in Blake's pocket.

Jo parted the curtains over the kitchen window and scanned the rapidly darkening street for signs of her husband. Dinner sat warming in the oven, rapidly approaching an uneatable dryness. Cooking had never been her strong point and was worse when it had to sit.

She released her breath when the light from the Harley shone through the window. It seemed as if Conley arrived later and later each night, tired, dirty, and often sporting new bruises which he refused to let her know how he'd gotten.

Feeling like a nagging housewife, Jo tossed down the dishtowel she'd been holding and stormed to the front door. Conley swept her into his arms and lifted her off her feet. "Where's Alex?"

Despite her annoyance at his lateness, she smiled. "Watching cartoons. Why?"

He set her back on her feet and ushered her into the kitchen. "Were you aware that your father owns a plot of land about twenty miles out of Prestige? And were you further aware that Blake is co-owner, along with your uncle Dave, and that they are building a row of tract homes?"

Jo shook her head. Her brow wrinkled. "So?"

"Basement tract homes."

"I still don't get where you're going with this."

"Ten years ago, a child went missing. The little girl was gone for weeks. Her body was later found in a creek. A creek that just happens to cut through your father's land."

Jo leaned against the table. "You believe that the children are held somewhere on that land."

"Yes. I also think they'll have to be moved soon. Before construction begins." He pulled her back into his arms and kissed her. "We're getting closer to solving this."

"You think the children are still there?"

"I'm praying they are. With me digging into places I'm not wanted, it'll have been difficult to sell them out from under my nose. I'm annoying a lot of people. I also think that they need to be kept for a good long while to enable the fear to help mold them into forgetting who they are. That wouldn't happen with only one or two nights in a hole."

"That's what scares me." Jo turned and moved to the oven. Her husband's constant digging into matters that alarmed the wealthy of Prestige was like a time bomb. Each question he asked was one click closer to detonation. But, she understood his need to help the children. She felt the same need to protect her son.

She couldn't imagine life without Conley. Two months ago, he'd been a stranger. Just another face at work. His digging around like a dog searching for a bone kept her anxious. Sleep didn't come easy for her. She lived in a constant state of tension.

Staying in Prestige caused regret as sharp as cancer to eat away at her. Fear for Conley and Alex ate at her constantly. Guilt, for wanting to leave when Conley's heart for finding the lost children was so noble, left her ashamed.

She knew her quietness troubled her husband. He worried about her, along with what he tried to do. And she still hadn't told him she loved him, adding more guilt to her rapidly overflowing cup. The reason why eluded her. She did love him. More than anything.

He'd bought her a Bible a few weeks before, and she'd strived to be consistent in her reading. Her knowledge of Conley's God lacked in so many areas. Yet the hours he was gone, although prime reading time, was too often spent with her searching the night for signs of the Harley roaring up the drive.

"Alex, dinner." She set the casserole dish in the center of the table. Conley placed a hand over hers.

"Are you all right?"

She forced a smile on her face as she caught sight of his newly skinned knuckles. "I'm fine. Better than you, obviously."

"It's nothing." He ruffled Alex's hair as the boy passed him. "How was your day, Squirt?"

"Boring. Mommy won't let me go to school or play outside."

"It's for your own safety, son." Jo spooned up a serving of chicken and rice and slopped the food messily on Conley's plate. "Someday things will settle down."

She decided to confront Conley about the scrapes on his hand, the bruised ribs from a week ago, and the fading black eye, after dinner. He always clammed up, refusing to give any details. Assuring her things were fine and not to worry. Well, not this time.

Dinner was silent. Broken only by Alex's chattering about the latest cartoon escapades of Spiderman, Superman, or some other super hero. When he'd finished eating, Alex kissed her cheek and dashed back to the living room.

Jo pushed away her plate. "Conley…" Confrontation was something she ran from normally. Even with someone as gentle as her husband, she had no idea how to make him talk to her. How to get him to open up when he wanted to keep things hidden. "Are you happy being married to me?"

His head jerked up. "I love you. I wouldn't want

to be anywhere else."

Tears welled in her eyes, despite her attempt to squelch them back. The last thing she wanted was for Conley to think she was using tears to get him to talk. How could anyone stay angry with this man?

"What's going on with you? Where do you disappear to every day? You roar out of here on your bike before I climb out of bed. You come home at least twice a week looking like you've been in a fight. You won't talk to me. I'm worried, Conley. We're married. You should share things with me."

He sighed and set his fork with careful precision on the edge of his plate. "I wanted to spare you. You're right. We're partners, and you deserve to know what I've been up to." He reached across the table and took her hands in his.

"I have been fighting. Chief Logan doesn't want me here. I'm getting too close to what this town's hiding. His boys get a little heavy handed a few times a week as a warning It's a lot like playground bullying."

Jo's heart stilled. "They'll kill you."

"No, they won't. They don't want another murder under their belt. They just want me to leave." He released her hands and stood. "I'm tough, Jo. I'll be fine."

"You're leaving again."

"Yes."

"And you won't tell me where."

"I'm sorry."

She waved aside his excuse. "I have a good idea

anyway."

He placed a kiss on the top of her head and left the house. She rose and watched out the window as he backed the Harley from the driveway. Why couldn't she be stronger? She'd been nothing but a weak coward for as long as she could remember. Maybe she *should* call on God to give her strength. Conley seemed to think that's where he got his.

*

From the concealing canopy of a low branched tree, Conley studied the chief of police's house across the street with the aide of binoculars. He'd watched Blake enter the house less than an hour ago. Nothing had happened since.

He hoped they would lead him to the children. Someone had to be caring for them. Starved, uncared for children wouldn't raise a lot of money on the black market. After two weeks, he prayed they were still in Prestige. Having them moved would make his search next to impossible.

A hunter's moon rose above the trees and lighted the neighborhood with a brilliant white light. He pushed the bike further into the shadows and settled in for a long wait.

He perked up at the sound of loud voices. Through the curtains he could make out the shadows of two people. They appeared to be shoving a third.

More shouts.

A scream.

A gunshot.

Minutes later, Chief Logan and Blake struggled to carry what appeared to be a large body wrapped in a sheet to the trunk of Blake's car. They dropped their burden. It landed with a dull thud to the concrete driveway.

Chief Logan cursed.

Blake hissed. "You aren't holding up your end. Do you expect me to carry this big lug myself?"

"I expect you to do as you're told. We wouldn't be in this mess if you'd taken care of that hippy, motorcycle riding, freak your wife married. Now, Sylvia's being all hysterical. Things have gotten messy. I don't like it."

"Sylvia will be fine. She knows what to do. Harold will keep her in line."

The two men hefted and tossed their burden in the trunk then slammed it closed.

Conley held his breath and froze. He prayed the shadows were enough to hide him. *Please God, don't let the moon reflect off the Harley's chrome*.

Doors slammed, and Blake's car pulled out of the driveway. Officer Logan took another glance up and down the street then hurried back into his house. Conley started the Harley and roared after Blake.

He followed the silver Mercedes for five miles before it turned off the highway and down a dirt road. The road was heavily laden with rocks and holes. Deciding to spare the bike, Conley stopped and slipped the Harley behind some thick brush. Still able to make out the tail lights of Blake's car, he ran in a crouch down the road.

With a stitch in his side, and breathing accelerated, Conley stopped and estimated he'd run about two miles before the car stopped fifty feet up the road. He balanced his hands on his knees and struggled to catch his breath.

Muffled cursing, grunts, and a slam. Conley inched closer.

The car was parked in front of a ramshackle cabin built before a pond. The cabin looked as if a stiff wind would blow it right into the water. A dock and boathouse, more dilapidated than the cabin, rose from the water. This, apparently, was Blake's destination.

Blake fished a key from the pocket of his pants, inserted it in a padlock on the sagging boathouse door, and dragged the sheet-covered body inside. Conley moved closer and stepped onto the dock, being careful to stifle his footsteps.

He snuck closer to peer in the grime-covered window. Blake stood over a hole in the floor, the wrapped body beside him. His hands rested on his knees and he struggled to regain his breath. "Stupid...man. Don't...know why...I have to...do this myself. It took two of us to get him in the car." Blake kicked the body.

The boards beneath his feet groaned and gave way when Conley ducked to avoid Blake seeing him. His arms wind-milled as he tried to grab the railing. The rotting wood broke beneath his grip. His head collided with a beam. He made one last desperate attempt to maintain his grasp on a wooden post. The dark water closed over his head, and his world turned black.

19

The clock on the kitchen wall chimed midnight, and Jo nursed her third cup of coffee. She struggled to maintain a positive attitude of prayer, and failed. She didn't even have the heart to move her sleeping son from the sofa to his bed upstairs.

In her gut, she knew something had happened to Conley.

When the clock struck one, she'd had enough. Shoving aside her coffee mug, she marched into the living room to gather her son. Alex laid on the couch, mouth slack, arms and legs flung wide. Jo hesitated for a moment at the sight of his sleepy abandon.

Concern over Conley's welfare spurred her to scoop Alex into her arms and carry him outside to the Mercedes. She placed him in the back seat, covered him with an afghan, then slid behind the wheel.

She had a cursory knowledge of the location of the

land Conley had mentioned, and, beneath a steadily rising wind and the beginning drops of rain, drove west. Past the chief of police's house. No lights burned in the windows although his squad car sat in the driveway. She couldn't help but wonder how a man such as himself could sleep at night.

Making a small detour, she passed her parent's house. No lights there, either. Blake's Mercedes sat silent in the driveway. She slowed and took a closer look. Mud caked the tread of Blake's tires. She was tempted to confront him. Force out of him whether he knew where Conley was. She'd bet he did.

Who was she trying to kid? She hadn't been able to stand up for herself when she'd been married to the man. What would cause her to be any different now? Once a coward, always a coward. Fear increasing, Jo drove faster and directed the car down the highway.

Cars sped past her, horns blaring as she cruised with the speed of a tortoise. Her gaze scanned the sides of the highway, looking for the signs of recently passing vehicles. Or a muddy road. When she'd reached the mental foothills of despair she spotted fresh tracks to her right.

Jo cut the lights and drove through the tree-shrouded darkness. She hunched over the steering wheel. Her eyes hurt from the strain. Bull frogs croaked from the pond behind the fallen down cabin. The rain increased and pimpled the surface of the water.

"Bingo," she whispered. "Alex. Baby. Wake up."

"Where are we?"

"Looking for Conley."

Alex leaned over the seat, hair mussed. "This looks like a haunted house."

"It does, doesn't it?" Jo studied the shadows and fallen timbers of the cabin. Lake water splashed against the pilings of the dock. "Grab the flashlight from the floor, would you, sweetie?"

He handed her the flashlight. She flicked it on, and exited the car. Her son climbed over the seat and stayed close to her side. With one hand gripping the light, and the other firmly grasping Alex's hand, Jo made her way down a slight incline to the dock.

Her feet sunk in the marshy ground around the pond, and she paused. No shout of alarm rang out. She tugged her son's arm and stepped out onto the wooden planks. The dock shifted beneath her feet. "Go back, Alex. Wait for mommy on the bank."

"No." He grabbed her hand. "Don't leave me. I'm scared."

"I have to." Jo untangled herself from her son's frantic grasp. "I have to see if Conley's in the boat house."

"Please, Mommy."

Jo sighed. Her gaze raked the area around them. They'd been separated too long. She couldn't leave him. "Okay. Hold tight. If we fall, you hold on to my hand, no matter what." *Please God, don't let them fall.* "Promise?"

"I promise."

The wind whipped their clothing, and Jo's hair

pulled free of its band. Howls issued from the cracks in the boards as the wind forced its way through. Water splashed against their feet. Lightening cracked overhead.

Jo's chest tightened. She patted her pocket, feeling the reassuring bulge of her inhaler. Alex's grip threatened to cut off the circulation in her fingers. *God, help. Where is he?* How would she find anybody in the approaching storm?

The dock pitched beneath her feet. Jo drew in a sharp breath and clutched at the railing. A splinter stabbed into her palm and she dropped the flashlight. It fell to the water below.

She dropped to her knees. Her gaze followed the beam of murky yellow light as it sank beneath the rippling water taking her courage with it. Alex screamed and hugged a post. Jo jerked to attention. Venturing onto the bucking wooden deck had not been a good idea.

She crawled toward her son, wrapped an arm around his waist, and dragged him behind her as she made her way back to the bank. Once they'd reached the blessed security of non-rolling land, she laid on her back, Alex beside her, and stared at the crackling lightening splitting the dark sky. There'd been no sign of Conley. Either she was too late or in the wrong place.

*

Conley swallowed a mouthful of fishy tasting water. For a moment he had no idea where he was. Then his memory returned, along with the pain in his head. The rocking of the beam beneath his arms threatened to send him back to the land of unconsciousness, and he fought against the urge to close his eyes and sink.

He blinked as his gaze fell on a light. The ray shone from the bottom of the lake, green and murky. He blinked again then looked above him to the dock. Jo? She belly-crawled above him and dragged something behind her. "Jo!"

Jo continued without him, finally collapsing on the bank of the lake. Conley shook his hair from his face and recognized the body lying beside her. He shook his head at her venturing out with Alex. At the same time, his heart swelled. She must care a lot about him to risk searching in this storm. And at the risk of her son.

The thought gave him strength, and he kicked against the waves. A roar behind him caused him to turn his head. The deck collapsed sending a wave of water over his head. His arms slipped from the beam, and he gulped more water as he went under.

He bobbed back to the surface. Another shake of his head left him dizzy, and he realized it wasn't only water running into his eyes, but blood as well. He went under again and opened his eyes, peering through the murky depths of the lake.

A face floated before him. There was a bullet hole in the center of the man's broad forehead. Despite this not being the first dead body Conley had ever seen, he couldn't hold back the shock. He backpedaled as fast as the water would allow. Planting his feet in the sandy bottom of the lake, he pushed upward and howled when his head broke the surface.

"Conley!" Jo fought her way through the water. By the time he'd made his way to where the water reached his waist, she'd slid beneath his right arm. "You're bleeding."

"And I've swallowed enough of this water to kill a horse." He yanked away from her, fell to his knees, and lost his dinner in the weeds beside the shack. Very manly.

Jo had taken off her tee shirt, wearing some little camisole thing now, and wrapped her shirt around his head. He wasn't so far gone as not to notice how his wife looked in wet satin.

"Come on." She tugged on his arm, cringing when lightening crashed overhead. "Let me help you to the car."

"My bike."

"You'll have to get it tomorrow. The storm's getting worse. I don't want Alex out here."

Conley glanced at the boy. At some time he'd gotten up and climbed into the dryness of the Mercedes. "Okay." His legs trembled beneath him, and he leaned heavily on Jo's thin shoulders. He tried taking some of his own weight, but she'd pull him back.

After a lurching march which left his stomach rolling as much as the pond had, Conley found himself in the front passenger seat of the car. Jo flicked the heater to high and Conley sat while his chills slowly subsided.

*

Jo didn't drive Conley home. Instead he found himself lying on a hospital bed in a cold and sterile emergency room after having his head x-rayed. He lay behind a green and white striped curtain and wished the room would stop spinning. Jo sat in a nearby chair with a sleeping Alex on her lap. She had to be freezing, but instead of wrapping herself with the extra blanket he'd requested, she'd wrapped her son.

Beneath finely arched brows, she glared at him. She'd been as caring as a loving mother toward him until she'd handed him over to the doctor's care, then what he could only describe as the Mr. Hyde side came out. She refused to talk to him. The silence in the room shook the walls until he couldn't take it anymore.

"Blake and Officer Logan killed a man tonight. His body is submerged in the waters beside the cabin."

Jo glanced at him, a question in her eyes.

"A big man. Blake had a hard time dragging him by himself. Bald. Clean shaven."

"Sounds like my uncle Dave." Jo fiddled with the blanket around Alex's face. "I wonder what he did to make the others turn on him. Maybe they'll be like piranhas and turn on each other. Then this will all be over. I can't say that I'm sorry he's dead."

"I'm sorry." Conley turned his head as slow as possible, fighting against the nausea the movement entailed. "I never expected you to come looking for me. Not that I'm not grateful. Lord, knows I am. If you hadn't, I'd be joining Dave at the bottom of that pond."

"I got lucky, Conley. What if I hadn't found you? What would Alex and I do?" She dabbed her eyes with a corner of the blanket.

"You do care." The realization made the knock on the head almost worth the pain.

"It's not funny."

"Mr. Hook." The doctor appeared, chart in hand. "You have a concussion and will need several stitches. My nurse will take care of that for you." He scribbled on a pad. "Here's something for the pain." The man glanced up. "Be careful where you choose to swim next time, won't you?" He smiled, slipped the chart in a slot beside the door, and left to be replaced with a matronly nurse armed with a tray.

Elephants stomped through Conley's stomach. If there was one thing in the world he hated, it was needles. If not for having to prove himself a tough man in jail, he never would've had the gumption to get his tattoos. The ridicule of fellow inmates goes a long way to spurring a person to making stupid decisions. "You aren't going to stick me with that are you?"

"Unless you want me to stitch your head without a local, I am." She set the tray on the rolling table and pulled it close to the bed. "Are you going to be a good boy, or do I need to call for someone to hold you down?"

Thirty minutes later, Conley found himself pushed in a wheelchair to the emergency entrance where Jo had pulled up the car and now held open the passenger side door. His forehead was numb, the stitches pulled his skin, and his headache had numbed to a dull pain behind his eyes. The parking lot lights of the hospital were too bright, and he closed his eyes. He opened them to the unpleasant sight of Officer Logan leaning against the outer brick wall of the building.

The officer uncrossed his arms and stepped forward until he stood before the wheelchair. "Heard you got your head bashed in. Mind telling me where this happened?"

"Fell down the stairs." Did the man suspect where Conley had been?

"No one struck you? You weren't provoked into a fight?"

"Look, Logan. Your men have been harassing me since I got here. It's no surprise to you. Why the concern all of a sudden?" Conley stood and leaned against the car.

"Just doing my job."

"There's always a first time." Conley slid into the passenger seat of the Mercedes and Jo closed the door. Was he fishing for information? Conley rested his head against the back of the seat and prayed he'd feel well enough tomorrow to scout the land surrounding the cabin.

20

Blake twirled his pen while Logan filled him in on Conley Hook's injuries. Minor, the man said. Blake hadn't been aware of anyone beating on the man last night. He usually knew about or at least ordered the events. Hook was proving stronger than he'd thought. So had Jocelyn. What happened to the submissive woman he'd trained? She had developed a backbone, and he didn't like it.

"You should have had him killed. I don't care what you think about his death raising more suspicions. The man has no family. I doubt he'd be missed." Blake clicked the ballpoint pen. "Other than Jocelyn, no one would care. And she's only doing this to get back at me for divorcing her. She'll come to her senses. If she doesn't…" He didn't want to think about the consequences if she didn't come back to him.

"Look, Blake, Harold is putting the pressure on me

to wrap these things up. He has buyers lined up. If Hook finds where we're holding…"

"He won't." The doorbell rang. "Someone's at the door, Logan. I'll talk to you tomorrow." He placed the phone back on its stand and waited for the housekeeper to send his guest to him.

Meredith waltzed into his office. Something black and filmy peeked past the last button on her overcoat. He smiled and moved to join her. He couldn't help but wish it was Jocelyn standing before him. Dave would have called him a fool for obsessing over a mere woman, but when a young man has the privilege of choosing his future wife, then having her molded to his own idea of perfection, well, there was no greater feeling in the world.

Now, an ex-con thought he could take all that hard work away from Blake and toss it away. Not if he could help it. Maybe he needed to put a bullet through the man's brain. No one would care enough to dig into the murder.

*

"No. Absolutely not." Jo couldn't believe Conley intended to leave the house after what happened last night. "You still have a pounding headache. Just take tonight off, pop a pill, and get some rest."

He speared her with his gaze. "There are children waiting to be found. I can't sit and let them wait any longer than necessary. You know what it was like. Think of your nightmares. Can you wish that on anyone?"

223　　·

"Then let me help." Jo squared her shoulders. "Tell me what to do. You can stay here with Alex." If she could only remember where she'd been held as a child. Most homes in Prestige had basements or root cellars. Looking for a hole in the ground would be like looking for that proverbial needle in a haystack. *Please, God, let me remember*.

"You wouldn't know where to begin." Conley grabbed his motorcycle helmet.

"I'll begin with my mother. If I put enough pressure on her, she'll have to cave." Jo glanced at her watch. "It's almost ten-thirty. She'll be sleeping, and I can catch her unaware."

"What about your father?"

Her heart leaped that Conley was considering her proposal. "It's Friday. He stays at the country club until at least midnight."

Conley dropped the helmet in a chair and lowered himself to the sofa. "The idea of you being out this late scares me, but not any more than the idea of getting on the back of my bike or behind the wheel of a car."

"Great." Jo planted a kiss on Conley's forehead, grabbed her purse from the foyer table, then headed to the garage. She'd been wanting to corner her mother again since hearing on the news about the last child disappearing from a truck stop. Her anxiety of Alex's safety had kept her chained to the house.

Prestige lay quiet beneath a three-quarter moon. Clouds, like pulled cotton, drifted in lazy groups across the sky and gave the town almost a fairy land glow. Despite the horrors of her childhood, Jo loved the little town. When everything was behind them, she hoped to remain and build a life with Conley. A normal life. One where she felt free to tell him she loved him. If he stayed after completing his quest.

She passed the skeletal remains of Blake's home. Fresh wood was piled at the perimeter of the lot. He was building another monstrosity to tower over the surrounding Victorian estates. Jo gave thanks that she lived on the opposite side of town.

The closer she got to her destination, the faster her heart beat. Swallowing against the dryness in her mouth, she pulled into her parents' driveway and cut the engine. The manicured lawns and welcoming atmosphere of the outside of the house gave no indication of the misguided lives inside. She took a deep breath. It was now or never.

Her gym shoes made no sound as she crept up the flagstone walk. No dogs barked. They wouldn't dare. Not in this neighborhood.

She'd never returned the key when she and Conley had moved out and she inserted it into the brass handle on the front door. With a glance behind her, she turned the key then pushed the door open.

At the end of the foyer and to her right sat her father's study. Visiting her mother could wait. Jo might not have another chance to snoop in the study. Keeping to the shadows, she made her way to the room. Double doors pushed open to reveal walls lined with books and a mahogany desk. A flat screen laptop took precedence on the highly polished surface.

She closed the door behind her and made her way to the computer. She knew it would require a password, yet the request made her groan anyway. To her left towered a five-drawer filing cabinet. The drawers were locked. She transferred her attention to the bookshelves. Could her father have a secret panel hidden behind one of the books? She pulled the books forward, one by one, before sliding them back into place with gentle thuds. Three thirds of the way around, she was rewarded with the sliding open of a wall safe.

A large padded envelope, along with several stacks of hundred dollar bills filled the small enclosure. Jo's heart beat so loud she was afraid her mother would hear upstairs and wake up to investigate. With a trembling hand she withdrew the manila envelope.

She lifted the flap and pulled out three 8 x 10 photos. Two were of the missing brother and sister. The third was of a red-haired girl around the age of thirteen. Jo gasped and stuffed the photos back into the envelope. Her breath caught in her throat. Did the photos mean the children were still close?

A footfall outside the door of the office spurred her into shoving the envelope back into the safe. As the doors opened, she ducked behind the floor-length curtains that covered French doors. She couldn't see through the thick brocade fabric. She concentrated on controlling her breathing. The door to the study banged open.

"Dave is dead." A sharp cry and it sounded as if someone was tossed onto the leather sofa on the other side of the room. Jo held her breath. "If you open your mouth, the same will happen to you."

"How can you say that? We've been married for forty years. Please, Harold."

"Forty years of listening to your harping. Wanting this, wanting that. Where do you think the money comes from? Now, you're starting to develop a conscience? We killed Dave for you, Sylvia. Don't forget it. You and your whining about his treatment of our daughter. Some things are better left alone!" The door to the office opened and slammed shut. Sylvia sobbed.

A guilty sense of relief coursed through Jo. Why had Sylvia turned against her brother? The clouds shifted, releasing the moon's brilliance.

"You can come out now." Sylvia sniffed. Jo stepped from her hiding place.

"How did you know I was there?"

Sylvia reached for a tissue from a wooden box on the coffee table. "Every time the moon came out from the clouds, I could see your silhouette. It's a good thing Harold's back was turned."

"Are you going to tell him?"

Sylvia shook her head. "I can't do this anymore, Jocelyn. I really can't."

"Why did they kill Dave?" Jo perched beside her mother.

"He was overstepping his boundaries where I was concerned. I belong to Harold. No one else, and sometimes my brother tended to forget."

The festered wound inside her burst, flooding her emotions. Jo tensed and clinched her fists. "But it was okay for a little girl to be passed around like a toy."

"There wasn't anything I could do about that." Sylvia raised red-rimmed, swollen eyes. "I tried and ended up, bruised and in bed for my trouble. One time, I was hospitalized for broken ribs."

"Where are the children?"

"I'm not sure. I think they're in a cellar near the lake…" Footsteps approached and paused outside the door.

Harold ordered someone to check the fence perimeter. "She's got to be here somewhere."

"Go. Now." Sylvia leaped from the sofa and shoved Jo toward the French doors. "If he finds you here, he'll hurt both of us."

Jo whirled and dove outside into the bushes.

"What are you doing, Sylvia? Close the door. You're letting in the cold air." From her position behind some juniper shrubs, Jo spotted Harold push past her wife and stare with narrowed-eyes into the night. After several tense minutes, he closed the doors and drew the curtains.

A flashlight beam cut across the lawn fifty yards from where Jo huddled. Prisms of light illuminated the arches of water from the sprinkler system. She scanned the lawn, then ran in a crouching run to the next set of sculpted bushes. She thanked God her parents didn't keep dogs. How had her father known she was on the premises? Oh, he'd seen the car. Stupid! But he always stayed late at the club on Fridays.

A shout almost made her jump upright. She clamped a hand over her mouth to choke back a scream and knelt in the damp dirt. Despite a chill in the air, her skin grew clammy with nervous perspiration. When the searchers rounded the house, she darted across the lawn, grabbed the top of the gate and struggled to pull herself over.

Her feet slipped on the iron bars. The top point stabbed her hand. A cry of pain escaped. The blood made the bars more slippery and tears of frustration welled. *Come on, Jo. You can do this.* She grunted, heaved, and landed in a heap on the other side of the fence. Alarms wailed from speakers positioned around the house. The cameras! She'd forgotten the surveillance system her parents had installed a few months before she'd fled. They'd have her every move on film.

21

Jo snuck through the back door, her bleeding hand cradled against her side. From the living room came sounds of the television. With her uninjured hand, she flicked on the kitchen light then made her way to the sink.

"What did you do?" Conley sat at the kitchen table, his head propped in his hands. She got the impression he'd been praying. She had the overwhelming urge to hide her hand behind her back. "Let me see," he said.

She held her hand in front of her. Blood dripped to the white floor tile. "I cut myself climbing over the fence."

Conley rose to his feet, keeping one hand on the table. "Was it worth it?"

"I think so." Jo grinned and allowed Conley to take her injured hand in his. He wet a dishtowel and swabbed at the cut. "I went into Harold's study and searched until I found his safe. There were pictures in there. Of the brother and sister. Ow!" She tried to pull away. Conley held firm.

"And a picture of a girl about thirteen, I'd guess. That means they still have them, right?"

"Possibly." With another towel, he wrapped her clean hand. "You should probably have stitches."

"Aren't you tired of the hospital?" Jo slipped her hand from his and reached above her head for a glass. "Anyway, there's more. I hid behind the curtains just in time to avoid being caught by my parents. My father yelled at my mother about Uncle Dave. He said they killed him for her. When he left, she almost told me where the children were hidden. The lake … something. I had to run out the back door when my father came in. He ordered someone to search the grounds. I got this climbing over the fence."

Conley beamed at her. "You did good. But I was worried sick the whole time you were gone."

"I didn't do that well. I forgot about the surveillance equipment. They'll know I opened the safe. They'll know I found the photos." Dread filled her. "My memory has to return, Conley, before it's too late."

"Are you praying about it? God reveals what we need when we need it." He wrapped his arms around her.

She reciprocated and laid her head on his chest. "I'm trying. I still have a hard time believing in a loving rather than a vengeful God. Especially with everything that's happened."

"Keep searching. He'll reveal himself." He kissed the top of her head. "Let's go to bed."

*

Conley laid in bed with Jo's head cradled on his arm. Despite his pounding headache, his thoughts whirled as fast as a desert dust devil. He replayed his conversation with Jo. Where was the closest lake? Could Sylvia have meant the pond? Did it even have a name? He wanted to wake Jo. Instead, he glanced at the clock. Two a.m. His questions could wait a few more hours.

Four hours later, Conley woke to the ringing doorbell and someone pounding on the front door. The sound of the shower told him Jo was in the bathroom. He groaned and climbed from bed to shuffle his way to the door.

Sylvia, clothed in a silk robe and pajamas, kept one finger on the bell while she pounded. Conley opened the door and held out his hands to catch her as she tumbled inside.

"You've got to help me. He'll kill me." A fresh bruise colored one side of her face.

Conley assisted her to the sofa and lowered her onto it. "Tell me what happened."

"I didn't know where else to go." Gone was the stylish, self-confident woman. No makeup covered her face. No stylish twist or braid for her hair.

"You're all right, Sylvia. We'll take care of you." He handed her a box of tissues.

"Harold knows Jo was in the house. I told him I

didn't tell her anything. That I told her to leave. I'm not sure he believes me." She blew her nose.

"He hit you?" Conley sat in the chair opposite her.

Sylvia waved him off. "It's not the first time. It's Harold's way of making a point. I'm sorry, Conley." She looked at him. "I've known all along what my husband was involved in, and my son-in-law. You're a good man. You didn't deserve the type of welcome we gave you."

"Apology accepted." Conley leaned back in his seat.

"I feel better than I have in years." She wiped her eyes. "You don't need to look so shocked. If I had to bottle that guilt inside me for one more day, I'd most likely kill myself. Have you ever felt that way?"

He shook his head and wished Jo would come back.

"You've never had the feeling of an immense burden being lifted?" It seemed as if once the woman's lips were unlocked, the words wouldn't stop.

"No, ma'am. I've made a habit of never doing anything I would be ashamed of."

"But you went to jail."

"As a juvenile. I made some mistakes. Let myself be led into some bad circles, but I wasn't ashamed. I thought I was being cool, but that's no longer who I am. Doing the right thing now doesn't mean you won't have to face the consequences of your actions."

"I'm willing to do anything not to feel like that again."

"Even to go so far as to tell me where your husband is hiding the children?"

22

Jo kept her back against the wall and her ears tuned to the conversation in the living room. Had Conley just saved her mother, not only physically, but spiritually? If only she could take the one step that would take her into a deeper relationship with Conley's God. She stepped around the corner and into the room when Conley asked where the children were.

Sylvia twisted the ties of her robe in her hands. "I want to help. I do. There is so much I need to make up for." She raised her head and looked at Jo. "But I don't know the exact location."

"Anything you can tell us is more than we know now." Conley waved Jo over and she perched on the arm of his chair. He slid an arm around her waist. She marveled at how safe a simple touch from him made her feel.

"You told me 'the lake' something," Jo

reminded her.

"The Lake Estates." Sylvia blurted the words. "The new development your father and Blake are building. The pit has always been on that land. I just don't know the exact spot." She scoffed. "Your father said not knowing was for my own protection."

"How large is that tract of land?" Conley said.

Sylvia shrugged. "Several hundred acres."

He removed his arm from Jo's waist and ran his hands through his hair. "It'll be impossible."

"Not if we can get Blake to take me there." Jo stood. "What can I do to infuriate him enough that he throws me in the pit? Then, I call you and you come and get me."

"Absolutely not." Conley's brow drew together. "Besides, Blake is too smart to let you carry a cell phone during a kidnapping."

"You're a private investigator, bug me." It would work. She knew it would. But how would they get Blake to take the bait? "I'll have to pretend to come to my senses and go back to him."

Conley bolted to his feet. "No."

"It'll work. Wire me and Alex. He's bound to take one of us."

"This is ridiculous!'

"It isn't." She laid her hand on his arm. "I'll snoop through his office. Either he'll catch me and be mad enough to punish me, or he'll take Alex." The thought grabbed her heart in a fist of ice. "Maybe we'll get lucky, and I'll find the location."

"No. We'll find another way. Blake is not that stupid."

Jo planted herself in front of Conley. "Then you'd better think of something, because one way or another I'm going through his office." She turned to her mother. "Where'd he move after the fire?"

"With your father and I." Sylvia fiddled with her robe.

"His office. Where's his office?"

"I don't know. He's been spending a lot of time with Logan. That's the house you should go through. He's the ring-leader in all this." She stared at Jo and Conley. "Do the two of you really think you can put a stop to this?"

"Yes." Jo grinned at Conley. "There you go." She glanced at her watch. Five a.m. "Tonight, I visit Logan's house."

"*We'll* visit Logan's house."

Sylvia stood. "You won't have a chance to do either if your father presses charges on you for breaking and entering." She tightened her sash. "Do you have an extra room where I can get a few hours of sleep? Then I'll leave and find a motel somewhere."

"New plan. You'll have to take Alex with you." Jo took Sylvia's elbow. "If you head to the valley, you'll have more places to hide. Go now."

"I know I have a lot to atone for, but may I at least borrow something to wear?"

Jo led her mother upstairs and into her walk-in-closet. Sylvia stopped a foot inside the door. "Jocelyn, my bathroom is bigger than this closet. And where are all your clothes?"

"Destroyed when Blake's house burned. I have plenty of clothes, mother. I'm a stay-at-home housewife. Conley and I aren't exactly the type of people invited to dinner parties."

"You were raised to present a certain standard. How will I find anything to wear in here?" Sylvia frowned and rang her fingers over the few blouses on hangars. She selected a deep blue sweater and cream pants. "These will have to do."

*

Jo fought back the tears of fear as Alex climbed into the car with Sylvia. Conley stood beside her, his hand on the small of her back. He stood rigid. His anger radiated from him in waves. If he'd ever resorted to acts of violence toward her, she'd be scared. They'd be having fireworks once they stepped back into the house.

She sniffed, gave Alex a final wave, then stiffened her spine and went inside to the living room. What they had planned was dangerous. Not only for her and Conley, but for Alex. She prayed it was all worth it. That God was on their side, leading them as he did the tribes of Israel long ago. She held up a hand to stop Conley as he opened his mouth.

"Just hear me out. You're still suffering the effects of your concussion. Blake and Logan might shoot you and ask questions later. With me, there's a chance of living if I'm discovered." Jo plopped onto the sofa.

Conley sat next to her and took her hands in his. "It's too dangerous. Alex needs his mother. *I* need you. If something happens…"

"We have to take that chance. If they've started building on that land, they'll move the children. Soon." She found it difficult to concentrate with him rubbing her hands. His touch soothed and excited her. Her hands went limp.

He pulled her forward until their foreheads touched. "Please?"

"I have to do this. I've been a frightened doormat for too long. Let me help you."

He sighed. "We'll do this together. I won't let you out of my sight."

"I don't want it any other way."

Conley released her and sat back against the sofa cushions. "Now, we just need a diversion to make sure Logan won't be home."

"An anonymous phone call?"

"I like the way your mind works." Conley picked up his phone, punched in a few numbers, then adopted a shrill tone, sounding like a frantic elder woman.

Laughing seemed inappropriate considering the circumstances. It was either that or cry, and she was done with crying.

23

Jo insisted on taking the Mercedes on their spying trip. She and Conley sat huddled in the front seat, hunkered down against the cold front sweeping through the state.

Wind whistled through the trees above the car and sent leaves skittering across the blacktop. Lights flicked on then off as Logan moved from one room of his house to the other. Blake was noticeably absent.

Conley held out his hand. "Let me use your cell phone. It doesn't look like he's going to leave anytime soon."

"Wait." Jo gripped his arm. "He's coming out."

Chief Logan pulled the collar of his bomber jacket around his neck and turned to lock the door. Then without glancing in either direction, he moved to his squad car. Leaves blew in a whirlwind, highlighted by the lights of his car as he drove down the street and around the corner.

"Okay," Jo said. "Let's go." She reached for the door handle

"Wait. We need to make sure he isn't back in a couple of minutes. If he isn't here in five, we'll go in."

They were the longest five minutes of Jo's life. The longer she sat, the more nervous she became. A twitch developed behind her right eye. She pumped her foot, ignoring the tapping against the car's dashboard. She'd never make a good private investigator. Too much sitting around doing nothing. Not to mention getting bashed in the head or shot at. She sighed.

"Stay beside me the entire time." Conley pushed open his door. "Do not get out of my sight. Clear?"

"Very." Jo sidled up next to him, still believing she should have come alone, but wise enough to see it was better to accept what he offered. "How are we going to get in?"

"I've got skills." Conley pulled a chiseled tool from a pocket in his jacket. He inserted the device into the door lock. "This is a disk tumbler lock. A little patience, a good ear, and...we're in." The lock disengaged with a click, and Conley pushed the door open.

They stepped into a dark house full of shadows and over-stuffed furniture. "Since he's a cop, won't he have an alarm system?" Jo clutched Conley's arm.

"I'm not seeing any signs of one. As chief-of-police, he probably feels pretty safe, especially in

Prestige." Conley moved his arm until he held Jo's hand. "You're trembling."

"I'm terrified. This is different than breaking into my parents' house."

"Come on. We don't know when he'll be back." Conley pulled her along behind him. They found the home office behind the last door on their right. Jo stepped inside and waited while Conley closed the door. He pulled two small flashlights from another pocket and handed one to Jo.

With the push of a button she illuminated the area around her. She shone her tiny beam across the wall and spotted a file cabinet. She tried the drawer. Locked. Conley lifted a paper weight from the desk and smashed it into the cabinet. The drawer flew open.

"They'll know we were here." Jo said.

Conley shrugged. "It'll be obvious once we have the children."

While Conley riffled through the desk, Jo flipped through file folders. Nothing about Lake Estates, children, or construction. "There's nothing here."

"Keep looking. Try the bookcase and the closet."

Besides the rustle of paper and the rapid beat of her heart, Logan's house remained silent. Jo ran her fingers over the spines of books in the case, expecting at any moment to discover a hidden passage or safe. Time ticked by, increasing her anxiety. She stepped past the window toward the closet. A tree branch scratched against the window. She choked back a scream.

"Jo?"

"Nothing. Just the wind."

Inside the closet, she searched the wall for a light switch and almost shouted with joy when she found one. A flick of the switch, and she clicked off her flashlight. Boxes lined the upper shelf of the closet. She counted twenty. She'd never get through them in time.

"Conley, help."

"Wow." He appeared at her side. "You start at this end. There's bound to be something here."

Box after box contained receipts, drawings, letters, etc. Anything and everything pertaining to construction or police work. Jo despaired.

"Here." Conley clutched a fistful of folded letters. "Names, dates; it's all here. Even a map. Thank you, God." He stepped back into the office and spread the parcel map on the desk. "Do you think X marks the spot?"

"Why would he do something so simple?" Jo peered over his shoulder.

"Not everyone would know what this X meant." He grinned at her. "Now, we can save them, Jo. We know exactly where to look."

"Very clever, Hook." Logan stood framed in the doorway, a revolver aimed at them. "You've proven a worthy adversary. Blake should've done away with you a long time ago." He swung the barrel of the gun toward Conley.

Jo shoved against Conley's shoulder.

Conley collapsed to the floor.

She screamed his name.

*

Fire seared through his shoulder. Conley groaned and moved to sit. His forehead banged against something above him. The drone of tires alerted him to the fact he was in the trunk of a car, bound hand and foot. Nothing new for him. He'd pray and wait for his opportunity.

Rocks hit the under carriage of the car. The vehicle bottomed out in what Conley guessed was pot holes. He suspected his destination was the boat house. Well, he'd already seen it and hadn't admired the view.

The car skidded to a stop. Dust crept into his prison. He clamped his lips tight against the sneeze and closed his eyes, remaining unresponsive.

"Let's get this over with." Blake grabbed Conley's ankles.

"You should have taken care of him weeks ago. Then our whole operation wouldn't be in jeopardy." Logan gripped Conley's shoulders. Pain radiated down his arm. By sheer will-power and prayer he kept his breathing low and even.

The two men dragged him to the dock and tossed him into the shallow water. The frigid water took his remaining breath away. Conley squirmed like a fish, struggling to reach the surface. He sank. His knee bashed against a rock on the bottom.

Fighting against approaching unconsciousness, Conley sawed the rope binding his wrists against the sharp edge of the rock. The murky water grew dimmer.

Despite the agony radiating through his upper body, he increased the motion of his hands.

His lungs burned before the fibers broke through, and he pulled himself hand over hand to the rotting beams above his head. He lay on the dock and gasped for air. Each breath torture. Each thought of what might be happening to Jo, sheer anguish.

With numb fingers, he struggled with the rope around his ankles. Violent shivers shook his frame, making him clumsy. Finally the ropes fell away. Free, he lurched toward the road, the picture of the map clear in his head.

24

Jo peered through the window as Logan and Blake tossed Conley's body into the water. She screamed his name through her gag and threw herself against the back passenger door of the car until her arm ached from the bruising. Her throat burned from unshed tears. The ropes binding her hands behind her back cut into her flesh.

"Sit back and shut up." Logan sneered at her as he slid behind the wheel. "We're going to take you somewhere familiar, girlie. It'll be like going home." He cackled and started the car. "Only this time, we don't know when we'll let you out."

Blake stared out the window, his jaw set in a firm line. He'd avoided Jo's eyes since Logan had called him. She shrieked and kicked the back of his seat. His head jerked forward. A curse escaped his lips.

Jo was no longer the meek woman he'd known

in the past. She wouldn't go down without a fight. Her heart lay like a cold stone at the realization of Conley being thrown away like yesterday's garbage. She choked back a sob. She'd never told him she loved him. But, she did. With everything in her. The realization of being too late ate at her, gnawing until her body ached with the pain.

She'd tried to shove him out of the way of the gun. Her world had fallen to the floor of Logan's office along with her husband. She failed.

Nightmarish visions of Conley drowning, trussed like an animal for roasting, haunted her. Her chest tightened. She focused on her breathing trying to stave off an asthma attack. The inhaler in her pocket poked her thigh, taunting her with its closeness.

Too soon, they stopped. The two men dragged her from the car. She struggled until they let her fall into a heap on the gravel road.

"Once we get her into the pit," Logan said. "We'll track down that traitor of a mother of hers and throw her in too. Harold will thank us. Then, we'll sell the kid."

"Let's just do this." Blake grabbed one of her arms.

Jo jerked away and tried to tell him she could walk under her own steam. Garbled, unintelligible words shoved through the gag.

Blake whipped the cloth from her mouth. "Do you have something to say, sweetheart?"

"You're a pig. Don't touch me."

Blake shoved his face inches from Jo's. "I have the power to save your life."

"I'd rather die."

Logan moved dead branches to reveal a wooden trap door. He swung it open.

Blake put his hand in the middle of Jo's back and shoved her into blackness. "Have it your way."

She fell into a thick inky darkness. Her head struck something hard. She lost consciousness.

*

Jo's shove saved Conley's life. Instead of a bullet hole, his side sported a painful, bleeding graze. He leaned against a tree and struggled to catch his breath. The Harley looked miles away instead of fifty feet. Thank God, they hadn't made it back to retrieve it from the bushes.

He shoved away from the rough bark of the oak and staggered down the road. Using the hand on his uninjured side, Conley fished the keys from his pocket. Still numb from cold, his fingers fumbled the key as he tried inserting it into the ignition.

The engine roared to life. Heart in his throat, Conley sped in the direction of the Lake Estates, praying he wouldn't be too late.

By the time he got to general area he believed the pit to be, night had fully fallen. He had nothing with him. No flashlight, no weapon. Nothing but his mind and skills. It truly would be a battle of him and God against evil minded men.

A scream drifted on a breeze. He was close. Closing his eyes, he listened, hoping for another cry. There! Jo called Blake's name.

Conley rolled the bike behind some bushes, then stared at the keys in his hand. With them poking between his fingers, he could form a claw. The only weapon he had.

Let's do this. He ran at a crouch in the direction he'd heard Jo's cry.

*

"You're a freak, Blake. An evil man." Jo stared at his dark form, outlined by the moon. From the bottom of the pit, he loomed over her. She remembered the terror that image used to instill. Not anymore. She waited while he closed the door.

"Ma'am, are you here to help us?" A young girl's voice came from Jo's left.

"I'm here to try." Jo slid her feet along the floor, trying to prevent from running face first into the wall. "My hands are tied, though. Do you think you could help me first?"

"Yeah." Fingers brushed Jo's skin. Several long minutes later, her hands were free.

"Is there anyone else down here?" She squinted, trying to make out shapes in the darkness.

"A boy and girl. They've been here longer than me and don't talk much."

"Have they hurt you?"

"A fat man tried, but when I bit him and kicked him in the gonads, he just hit me and threw me back in here to learn a lesson. Said he'd teach me later but he hasn't been back."

A nervous giggle erupted. "Good for you, sweetie.

What's your name?"

"Heather."

"I'm Jo. Let's see about getting out of here."

"I've started digging notches in the dirt, but I'm not making a lot of progress, and my fingernails are broken."

A young girl ten times stronger than Jo had ever been. Maybe that's why the kidnapping ring chose younger children. Less chance of them fighting back. If only Conley were there to help them. She'd have to give into her grief later. Now, she needed to get the children free and to a neighboring town. A place where the authorities would listen to them.

"Are there a lot of bugs down here?"

"Not really," Heather answered. "A few, but not too bad. I don't mind them. Why?"

"When I was little, the place they kept me was full of bugs. I still have nightmares." Jo shuddered. At least these children didn't suffer the same horrors she had.

She ran her hands over the walls, amazed at how much progress Heather had made. There were notches two feet up. Jo gripped one above her head and started to climb. Too short. One foot kept her from touching the door and freedom.

She started digging, biting back the pricks of pain that came with broken fingernails and splinters in her skin. Heather had dug for days. Jo could dig for one.

Her feet slipped, sending her to the floor in an aching huddle. *Come on, God, a little help here for me and the kids.*

"That happens sometimes," Heather said. She touched Jo's shoulder. "Want me to balance you? I could put my hands against your bottom for leverage. I know it's personal, but I'll do anything to go home."

"Sweetheart, me too. Touch away." Jo climbed back up and smiled when Heather cupped her bottom. *Oh, Conley, this would bring a grin to your face.*

The latch opened. Moonlight spilled in.

"Hey, good-looking." Conley's gorgeous face peered down. "Who's that with you?"

"You're alive!" Her heart leaped. "Pull me out."

"Hold on. There's a ladder. Move out of the way."

Seconds later, the ladder hit the ground with a thud. Jo waved the two silent children forward and they scurried up the ladder after Heather. The poor babies. Shock registered on their faces. Jo prayed they'd find the counseling they needed and leave this horror behind them.

"Blake and Logan are gone. We have to find them," she said.

"Let's get these little ones somewhere safe first." Conley scratched his head. "All I have is the motorcycle."

"Then, go," she said. "We'll hide in the woods while you go get help."

She could see his reluctance. She felt the same. Cupping his face, she kissed him, putting in all the emotion she'd held at bay for so long. "Go. I love you, Conley Hook. Come back for me."

*

"I will. I promise." He turned and sprinted for the bike while she and the children dashed for the trees. Her declaration spurred him on, despite the blood soaking his shirt. Knowing she relied on him to save her helped him ignore the pain.

A mile down the road, highlights pierced the night. Conley groaned as the car passed then circled back. He'd never outrun them. But, he could try.

Where was the closest populated area? He needed a phone. At the least, he needed witnesses. Blake and Logan wouldn't kill him in front of people. There! A gas station sign called to him like a lover. He raced toward it. A glance over his shoulder showed he'd barely make it before the car hit him.

Conley hit loose gravel before the concrete lot of the station and laid the bike. Rolling, he felt his flesh tear. He'd have a major case of road rash if he survived. He fell into a ditch and folded into a ball, struggling to catch his breath. The longer he stalled his death, the more time Jo had to get the children to safety.

Death had no hold over him. Although he would like some time with Jo and Alex, he wasn't afraid when God called him home. But, it would be nice for death not to come at the hands of men like those two.

He forced himself to his knees and crawled toward the station building, using the ditch as cover for as long as possible. When he reached pavement again, he lurched to his feet and stumbled toward the door. An open sign welcomed him with the promise of rescue.

He shoved himself. "Call 9-1-1."

The young man behind the counter pointed over his shoulder. "But there's a cop right behind you."

"He's dirty!" Conley dove over the counter, praying the store had a gun. There! Thank you, God. "Get down, son. This is going to get ugly."

The boy cursed and ran for a back room. "Take whatever you want!"

Conley grabbed the pistol and checked the clip. Three bullets. Well, he only needed two. "Stop right there," he called through a gap in the counter. "I've got a gun and I will not hesitate to shoot you."

"Settle down, Hook." Logan waved for Blake to circle around the counter. "We don't want a gunfight. All we want is for you to go away and leave us alone. Forget about Prestige."

"I'm afraid I can't do that. What you're doing is evil."

"By your estimates." Logan pulled his weapon from his holster. "Guess I'll have to shoot you through that cheap plywood then. Won't take much explaining to tell people how you were killed in a failed robbery. An ex-con like you?" He shot through the counter.

"I will not let you kill me." Conley pulled the trigger. His shot caught Logan in the neck. The next shot took Blake in the leg. The last one, through the heart. He hated taking a life, much less two, but Jo and those children were more important than these two. God forgive him, but these men had left a path of destruction that couldn't be undone. The authorities could deal with Jo's father.

It was done. He laid back and closed his eyes as sirens wailed.

25

"Mrs Hook!"

Jo tightened her hold on the children and pressed farther back into the bushes.

"City of Roscoe police, ma'am. Come out!"

"Are they telling the truth?" Heather's eyes reflected the moon's glow.

"I don't know. I thought for sure my husband would come back for us." Unless he couldn't. Her eyes burned, and she ducked her head.

What if they'd failed? What if Conley lay dead? Alex captured? Remaining hidden would not answer any of her questions. "Stay with the younger kids." Jo stepped out of the bushes.

Three men in police uniform wandered the meadow with flashlights. They called her name again.

"I'm here." Jo waved her arms. "Here!" Alex needed her, whether Conley lived or not. Somehow, Jo would survive. With God's help, she would go on. Still waving her arms, she fell to her knees, soaking the fabric of her pants.

The officers rushed toward. One called for an ambulance.

"The children are in the woods. They're all right." Jo covered her face and sobbed. "I want to go home."

"We'll take you soon enough, Mrs. Hook." An officer helped her to her feet. "But, we thought you'd want to see your husband first."

"Conley? He's alive? Why isn't he here?" She stared into the man's face, unable to believe his words.

"He's injured, but alive." The officer grinned. "Thanks to the two of you, so are these children."

"My ex-husband? Logan?" Dare she believe it was over?

"Dead. Mr. Woodward is in custody, and Mrs. Woodward is caring for your son in your home. Please, Mrs. Hook, let me take you to the hospital, have you checked over, and let you see your husband."

She blinked away the tears. "I'd like nothing more."

*

Conley groaned and opened his eyes. What he wouldn't give for a drink? He turned to press the button for the nurse.

"Good morning." Jo smiled and moved toward the bed. "You, my husband, are a hero." She laid a newspaper across his stomach. "You made the front page."

He glanced at the headline and grinned. Man and

Wife Save Kidnapped Children. "Looks like we're both heroes. Come over here and give me a kiss."

"I'd like nothing better." She pressed her sweet mouth against his. "I'd like nothing better than to kiss you for the rest of my life." Sighing, she laid her cheek against his. "Oh, Conley, I've been a damaged fool. I love you with every breath I take."

"Sweetheart, God and I would love nothing more than to help you heal. Let's get me out of here and go get Alex. Our family needs to be together." He sat up and tossed aside the thin hospital blanket. He held out his hand for her to take.

She slipped her hand into his and grinned. "Yes, let's go home and start our new life."

The End

ABOUT THE AUTHOR

Multi-published and Best-Selling author Cynthia Hickey had three cozy mysteries and two novellas published through Barbour Publishing. Her first mystery, Fudge-Laced Felonies, won first place in the inspirational category of the Great Expectations contest in 2007. Her third cozy, Chocolate-Covered Crime, received a four-star review from Romantic Times. All three cozies have been re-released as ebooks through the MacGregor Literary Agency, along with a new cozy series, all of which stay in the top 50 of Amazon's ebooks for their genre. She has several historical romances releasing in 2013 and 2014 through Harlequin's Heartsong Presents. She is active on FB, twitter, and Goodreads. She lives in Arizona with her husband, one of their seven children, two dogs and two cats. She has five grandchildren who keep her busy and tell everyone they know that "Nana is a writer". Visit her website at www.cynthiahickey.com

Made in the USA
Lexington, KY
29 November 2014